AMONG THE IMPOSTORS

MARGARET PETERSON
HADDIX

Simon & Schuster Books for Young Readers
New York   London   Toronto   Sydney

With thanks to Erin Esmont Rabinowitz for her helpful suggestions

SIMON & SCHUSTER BOOKS FOR YOUNG READERS

 An imprint of Simon & Schuster Children's Publishing Division
1230 Avenue of the Americas, New York, New York 10020

Text copyright © 2001 by Margaret Peterson Haddix
All rights reserved including the right of reproduction in whole or in part in any form. SIMON & SCHUSTER BOOKS FOR YOUNG READERS is a trademark of Simon & Schuster. Book design by Heather Wood. The text for this book is set in Elysium. Printed in the United States of America

20 19 18 17 16

Library of Congress Cataloging-in-Publication Data Haddix, Margaret Peterson.
Among the impostors / Margaret Peterson Haddix.
p. cm.
Sequel to: Among the hidden.
Summary: In a future where the law limits a family to only two children, third-born Luke has been hiding for the entire twelve years of his life, until he enters boarding school under an assumed name and is forced to face his fears.
ISBN-13: 978-0-689-83904-7 (ISBN-10: 0-689-83904-9)
[1. Fear-Fiction. 2. Interpersonal relations-Fiction. 3. Science fiction.] I. Title.
PZ7.H1164 Ap 2001   [Fic]-dc21   00-058325
0417 FFG

For Connor

CHAPTER ONE

S ometimes he whispered his real name in the dark, in the middle of the night.

"Luke. My name is Luke."

He was sure no one could hear. His roommates were all asleep, and even if they weren't, there was no way the sound of his name could travel even the short distance to the bed above or beside him. He was fairly certain there were no bugs on him or in his room. He'd looked. But even if he'd missed seeing a microphone hidden in a mattress button or carved into the headboard, how could a microphone pick up a whisper he could barely hear himself?

He was safe now. Lying in bed, wide awake while everyone else slept, he reassured himself of that fact constantly. But his heart pounded and his face went clammy with fear every time he rounded his lips for that "u" sound—instead of the fake smile of the double "e" in Lee, the name he had to force himself to answer to now.

It was better to forget, to never speak his real name again.

But he'd lost everything else. Even just mouthing his

name was a comfort. It seemed like his only link now to his past, to his parents, his brothers.

To Jen.

By day, he kept his mouth shut.

He couldn't help it.

That first day, walking up the stairs of the Hendricks School for Boys with Jen's father, Luke had felt his jaw clench tighter and tighter the closer he got to the front door.

"Oh, don't look like that," Mr. Talbot had said, pretending to be jolly. "It's not reform school or anything."

The word stuck in Luke's brain. Reform. Re-form. Yes, they were going to re-form him. They were going to take a Luke and make him a Lee.

It was safe to be Lee. It wasn't safe to be Luke.

Jen's father stood with his hand on the ornate doorknob, waiting for a reply. But Luke couldn't have said a word if his life depended on it.

Jen's father hesitated, then pulled on the heavy door. They walked down a long hallway. The ceiling was so far away, Luke thought he could have stood his entire family on his shoulders—one on top of the other, Dad and Mother and Matthew and Mark—and the highest one still would barely touch. The walls were lined, floor to ceiling, with old paintings of people in costumes Luke had never seen outside of books.

Of course, there was very little he'd ever seen outside of books.

He tried not to stare, because if he really were Lee, surely everything would look familiar and ordinary. But that was hard to remember. They passed a classroom where dozens of boys sat in orderly rows, everyone facing away from the door. Luke gawked for so long that he practically began walking backwards. He'd known there were a lot of people in the world, but he'd never been able to imagine so many all in one place at the same time. Were any of them shadow children with fake identities, like Luke?

Jen's father clapped a hand on his shoulder, turning him around.

"Ah, here's the headmaster's office," Mr. Talbot said heartily. "Just what we were looking for."

Luke nodded, still mute, and followed him through a tall doorway.

A woman sitting behind a mammoth wood desk turned their way. She took one look at Luke and asked, "New boy?"

"Lee Grant," Jen's father said. "I spoke with the master about him last night."

"It's the middle of the semester, you know," she said warningly. "Unless he's very well prepared, he shan't catch up, and might have to repeat—"

"That won't be a problem," Mr. Talbot assured her. Luke was glad he didn't have to speak for himself. He knew he wasn't well prepared. He wasn't prepared for anything.

The woman was already reaching for files and papers.

"His parents faxed in his medical information and his

insurance standing and his academic records last night," she said. "But someone needs to sign these—"

Jen's father took the stack of papers as if he autographed other people's documents all the time.

Probably he did.

Luke watched Mr. Talbot flip through the papers, scrawling his name here, crossing out a word or a phrase or a whole paragraph there. Luke was sure Jen's father was going too fast to actually read any of it.

And that was when the homesickness hit Luke for the first time. He could just picture his own father peering cautiously at important papers, reading them over and over before he even picked up a pen. Luke could see his father's rheumy eyes squinted in concentration, his brow furrowed with anxiety.

He was always so afraid of being tricked.

Maybe Jen's father didn't care.

Luke had to swallow hard then. He made a gulping noise, and the woman looked at him. Luke couldn't read her expression. Curiosity? Contempt? Indifference?

He didn't think it was sympathy.

Jen's father finished then, handing the papers back to the woman with a flourish.

"I'll call a boy to show you your room," the woman said to Luke.

Luke nodded. The woman leaned over a box on her desk and said, "Mr. Dirk, could you send Rolly Sturgeon to the office?"

Luke heard a roar along with the man's reply, "Yes, Ms. Hawkins," as if all the boys in the school were laughing and cheering and hissing at once. Luke felt his legs go weak with fear. When this Rolly Sturgeon showed up, Luke wasn't sure he'd be able to walk.

"Well, I'll be off," Jen's father said. "Duty calls."

He stuck out his hand and after a moment Luke realized he was supposed to shake it. But he'd never shaken hands with anyone before, so he put out the wrong hand first. Jen's father frowned, moving his head violently side to side, and glaring pointedly at the woman behind the desk. Fortunately, she wasn't watching. Luke recovered. He clumsily touched his hand to Jen's father's.

"Good luck," Jen's father said, bringing his other hand up to Luke's, too.

Only when Mr. Talbot had pulled both hands away did Luke realize he'd placed a tiny scrap of paper between Luke's fingers. Luke held it there until the woman turned her back. Then he slid it into his pocket.

Jen's father smiled.

"Keep those grades up," he said. "And no running away this time, you hear?"

Luke gulped again, and nodded. And then Jen's father left without a backward glance.

CHAPTER *TWO*

L uke wanted to read the note from Mr. Talbot right
away. He was sure it would tell him everything—
everything he needed to know to survive Hendricks
School for Boys. No—to survive anything that might come
his way in this new life, outside hiding.

It was just one thin scrap of paper. Now that it was in
his pocket, Luke couldn't even feel it there. But he had
faith. Jen's father had hidden Luke from the Population
Police, double-crossing his own employer. He'd gotten
Luke his fake I.D., so he could move about as freely as anyone else, anyone who wasn't an illegal third child. Jen's
father had risked his career helping Luke. No, it was more
than that—he'd risked his life. Surely Mr. Talbot would
have written something incredibly wise.

Luke slid his hand into his pocket, his fingertips touching
the top of the note. Ms. Hawkins was looking away. Maybe—

The door opened behind Luke. Luke jerked his hand out
of his pocket.

"Scared you, didn't I?" a boy jeered. "Made you jump."

Luke was used to being teased. He had older brothers,

after all. But Matthew and Mark's teasing never sounded quite so mean. Still, Luke knew he had to answer.

"Sure. I'm jumpy like a cat," Luke started to say. It was an expression of his mother's. Being cat-jumpy was good. Like being quick on his feet.

Just in time, Luke remembered he couldn't mention cats. Cats were illegal, too, outlawed because they might take food that was supposed to go to starving humans. Back home, Luke had seen wild cats a few times, stalking the countryside. Dad had liked having them around because they ate rats and mice that might eat his grain. But if Luke were really Lee Grant, filthy-rich city boy, he wouldn't know a thing about cats, jumpy or otherwise.

He clamped his mouth shut, closing off his "Sure—" in a wimpy hiss. He kept his head down, too scared to look the other boy right in the eye.

The boy laughed, cruelly. He looked past Luke, to Ms. Hawkins.

"What's wrong with him?" the boy asked, as if Luke weren't even there. "Can't talk or something?"

Luke wanted Ms. Hawkins to stick up for him, to say, "He's just new. Don't you remember what that's like?" But she wasn't even paying attention. She frowned at the boy.

"Rolly, take him to room one fifty-six. There's an empty bed in there. Just put his suitcase down. Don't waste time unpacking. Then take him back to Mr. Dirk's history class with you. He's already behind. Lord knows what his parents were thinking."

Rolly shrugged and turned around.

"I did not dismiss you!" Ms. Hawkins shrieked.

"May I be dismissed?" Rolly asked mockingly.

"That's better," Ms. Hawkins said. "Now, get. Go on with you."

Luke picked up his suitcase and followed, hoping Rolly's request for dismissal would work for both of them. Either it did, or Ms. Hawkins didn't care.

In the hallway, Rolly took big steps. He was a good head taller than Luke, and had longer legs. It was all Luke could do to keep up, what with the suitcase banging against his ankles.

Rolly looked back over his shoulder, and started walking faster. He raced up a long stairway. By the time Luke reached the top, Rolly was nowhere in sight.

"Boo!"

Rolly leaped out from behind the newel post. Luke jumped so high, he lost his balance and teetered on the edge of the stairs. Rolly reached out, and Luke thought, *See, he's not so bad. He's going to catch me.* But Rolly pushed instead. Luke fell backwards. He might have tumbled down all the stairs, except that Rolly's push was crooked, and Luke landed on the railing. Pain shot through his back.

Rolly laughed.

"Got you good, didn't I?" he said.

Then, strangely, he grabbed Luke's bag and took off down the hall.

Luke was afraid he was stealing it. He galloped after Rolly.

Rolly screamed with laughter, maniacally.

This was not what Luke had expected.

Rolly dodged around a corner and Luke followed him. Rolly discovered a secret about Luke's bag that Luke had missed—it was on wheels. So Rolly could run at full-speed with the bag rolling behind him. He careened this way and that, the bag zigzagging from side to side. Luke got close enough to tackle it if he wanted, but he hesitated. If the bag had been full of his own clothes, all the hand-me-down jeans and flannel shirts he'd gotten after Matthew and Mark outgrew them, he would have leaped. But the bag held Baron clothes, stiff shirts and shiny pants that were supposed to make him look like Lee Grant, instead of Luke Garner. He couldn't risk ruining them. He focused on Rolly instead. Instinctively, Luke dove over the bag to catch Rolly's legs. It was like playing football. Rolly fell to the ground with a crash.

"Just what is the meaning of this?" a man's voice boomed above them.

Rolly was instantly on his feet.

"He attacked me, sir," Rolly said. "I was showing the new boy his room and he attacked me."

Luke opened his mouth to protest, but nothing came out. He'd learned that from Matthew and Mark: Don't tattle.

The man looked dismissively from Rolly to Luke.

"What is your name, young man?"

Luke froze. He had to stop himself from saying his real name automatically. Then he had a split second of fearing he wouldn't be able to remember the name he was supposed to use. Was he taking too long? The man's glare intensified.

"L-L-Lee. Lee Grant," Luke finally stammered.

"Well, Mr. Grant," the man snapped. "This is a fine way to begin your academic career at Hendricks. You and Mr. Sturgeon each have two demerits for this disgraceful display. You may report to my room after the final bell to do your time."

"But, sir, I told you," Rolly protested. "He attacked me."

"Very well, Mr. Sturgeon. Make that three demerits for each of you."

"But—" Rolly was undeterred.

"Four."

Rolly was going to complain again. Luke could tell by the way he was standing. But the man turned away and began walking down the hall, as if Rolly and Luke were both too unimportant to bother with, and he'd wasted enough time already.

Luke's head swam with questions. What were demerits? When was final bell? Where was this man's room? Who was he, anyway? Luke tried to muster up the nerve to call after the man—or to ask Rolly, which seemed even more dangerous. But then he was blindsided with a shove that sent him crashing into the wall.

"Fonrol!" Rolly exploded.

Luke slumped against the wall. His shoulder throbbed. Why did Rolly seem to hate him so much?

"Well, come on, you little exnay," Rolly taunted. "Want to get demerits from Mr. Dirk, too?"

He stepped backwards, tugging on Luke's suitcase. Then he shoved it through a nearby doorway. Luke looked up and saw 156 etched on a copper plaque on the door. Relief overwhelmed him. Finally something made sense. This was his room. The rest of the day would be horrible—he'd already resigned himself to that. But eventually it would be night, and he'd be sent to bed, and he could come to this room and shut the door. And then he could read the note from Jen's dad, if he didn't get a chance to read it before bedtime. Come nightfall, he'd know everything and be safe, alone in his own room.

Imagining the haven that awaited him in only a matter of hours, he got brave enough to peek around the corner.

The room held eight beds.

Seven of them were made up, with rich blue spreads stretched tautly from top to bottom. Only one, a lower bunk, was covered just by sheets.

Luke felt as desolate as that bed looked. He knew it was his. And he knew he wouldn't get to be alone in this room.

He probably wouldn't be safe, either, not if any of his seven roommates were anything like Rolly.

He edged his hand into his pocket, his fingers brushing the note from Jen's dad. What if he just pulled it out and read it now, right in front of Rolly?

He didn't dare. The way the last ten minutes had gone, Rolly would probably rip the note to shreds before Luke even had it completely out of his pocket.

And Jen's dad had acted like it was secret. If Ms. Hawkins wasn't supposed to see it, there was no way Rolly could be trusted.

Rolly hit Luke on the shoulder.

"Tag! You're it!" he hollered, and took off running. Panicked, Luke chased after him.

CHAPTER THREE

Luke managed to keep up with Rolly only because Rolly slowed to a dignified walk when he began passing classrooms instead of sleeping quarters. But it was a fast dignified walk, and Luke was terrified that Rolly might dart around a corner unexpectedly and disappear. Then Luke would be totally lost. So Luke dared to jog a little, hoping to keep pace.

A tall, thin man with a skimpy mustache came out of one of the rooms as Luke passed by.

"Two demerits, young man," he said to Luke. "No running allowed. You know the rules."

Luke didn't, and didn't have the nerve to say so.

Rolly smirked.

The thin man went back into his classroom. Luke knew he'd have to risk asking Rolly a question.

"Wha—" he began. But just then Rolly opened a tall, wooden door to one side of the hall and slipped through. Luke's reflexes weren't fast enough. The door shut behind Rolly and then Luke had to fumble with the knob. It was ornate and gold, and had to be turned further to the right than all the doorknobs at home.

Home . . .

For the second time in less than an hour, Luke was overcome with an almost unbearable wave of home-sickness.

Stupid, Luke chided himself. *How can you be homesick for doorknobs?*

Blinking quickly, he shoved on the door and it gave way. Blindly, he stepped in.

He was at the back of a huge classroom. Boys sat in row upon row upon row, dozens of them, it seemed to Luke, all the way to the front of the room. There, the tall, thin man who'd just given Luke demerits was writing on the wall.

Or was it the same man? Luke squinted, confused. Oh. There was a door at the front of the room, too. That was the door the man had used. But had Luke and Rolly really walked so far between the doors? Suddenly, Luke wasn't sure of anything.

Luke scanned the row of boys in front of him, looking for Rolly. He was supposed to stay close to Rolly, so that's what he'd do. But now he couldn't even remember if Rolly had brown hair or black, short or long, curly or straight. He'd really never looked that closely at Rolly, just followed him and gotten beat up by him. Any of the heads in front of him might belong to Rolly.

The man at the front of the class turned around.

"And the Greeks were—sit down—" he interrupted himself impatiently.

MARGARET PETERSON HADDIX

He was looking at Luke.

"M-Me?" Luke squeaked. "W-Where should I sit?"

His voice wasn't much more than a whisper. There was no way the man could have heard him, all the way at the front of the room. Probably the boy sitting a foot away hadn't even heard him. But suddenly every boy in the room turned around and stared at Luke.

It was awful. All those eyes, all looking at him. It was straight out of Luke's worst nightmares. Panic rooted him to the spot, but every muscle in his body was screaming for him to run, to hide anywhere he could. For twelve years—his entire life—he'd had to hide. To be seen was death. "Don't!" he wanted to scream. "Don't look at me! Don't report me! Please!"

But the muscles that controlled his mouth were as frozen as the rest of him. The tiny part of his mind that wasn't flooded with panic knew that that was good—now that he had a fake I.D., the last thing he should do was act like a boy who's had to hide. But to act normal, he needed to move, to obey the man at the front and sit down. And he couldn't make his body do that, either.

Then someone kicked him.

"Ow!" Luke crumbled.

Rough hands jerked him backwards. Miraculously, he landed on the corner of a chair, barely regained his balance, and managed not to fall completely. He slid to his right and was solidly in the seat.

"*Thank* you," the man at the front said with exaggerated,

mocking gratitude. "See me after class. As I was saying before I was so rudely interrupted, the Greeks were quite technologically advanced for their time. . . ."

Then Luke could no longer hear the man's words over the buzzing in his ears. His heart kept thumping hard, as if it, at least, still thought Luke would be wise to run. But Luke resolutely gripped the edge of the chair. He was acting normal now. Wasn't he? The boys who had been staring at him slowly began turning back to face the teacher again. Luke wiped sweat from his forehead and looked around for whoever had kicked and pulled and shoved him. Had they been trying to help him? Luke desperately wanted to believe that. But all the boys near him were looking at the teacher, nonchalantly, as though Luke weren't even there. And if they'd been trying to help, wouldn't they be trying to catch Luke's eye, to get him to say thanks?

Luke really didn't know. He knew how his family would act—Mother and Dad, Matthew and Mark. Mother and Dad would never kick him, and his older brothers would be poking him now, taunting him, "Want us to kick you again?"

The only other people Luke had ever met before today were Jen's dad—who was practically as big a mystery as the boys sitting beside him now—and Jen. And Jen would . . .

Luke couldn't bear to think about Jen.

A bell rang suddenly, and it was such an alarming sound that Luke's heart set to pounding again.

"Remember! Chapter twelve!" the teacher called as all the boys scrambled up.

Luke meant to go see the teacher, as he'd been instructed. This had to be the end of the class. But the tide of boys swept him out the back door of the classroom before he quite knew what was happening. By the time he got his feet firmly on the ground, and felt like he might be able to break away, he was around a corner and down another hall. He fought his way back to what he thought was the original hallway. But then he couldn't figure out which way to turn. He looked all around, frantically searching for either the teacher or Rolly—as nasty as he'd been, Rolly was at least sort of familiar. But all the faces that flowed past him were strangers'.

Of course, the way Luke's mind was working, both Rolly and the teacher could have paraded past Luke five times and he might not have even recognized them.

The crowd in the hall was thinning out. Luke began to panic again.

"Get to class," an older boy standing nearby ordered him.

"Where?" Luke said. "Where's my class?"

The boy didn't hear him. Luke thought about asking again, louder, but the boy seemed to be some sort of guard, someone in charge, like a policeman.

Like the Population Police.

Luke put his hand over his mouth and veered away, down another hall. Another bell rang and boys started running, desperate to get into their classrooms. Hope-lessly, Luke followed a group of three or four through a doorway, into another classroom. At least, he thought it was another classroom. For all he knew, he might have circled around and gone into the same one all over again. Maybe that was good. Maybe after class this time, he could make it up to talk to the teacher—

It was a short, fat man who stood up to talk this time. As confused and panicky as Luke felt, even he could tell it wasn't the same teacher.

Luke hastily sat down, terrified of drawing attention to himself again. He resolved to listen carefully this time, to pay attention and learn. He owed it to everyone—to Mother and Dad, to Jen's father, even to Jen herself.

It was ten minutes before he realized that the man at the front was speaking some other language, one Luke had never heard before and didn't have a prayer of under-standing.

CHAPTER *FOUR*

When the bell rang after this class, Luke didn't even try to go against the crowd. This time the flow of traffic carried him to a huge room with tables instead of desks, and bookshelves instead of portraits on the wall. All the other boys sat down and pulled out books and paper and pens or pencils.

Homework. They were doing homework.

Luke felt brilliant for figuring that out. How many times had he watched his older brothers groan over math problems, stumble over reading assignments, scratch out answers in history workbooks? Matthew and Mark did not like school. Once, years ago, Luke had been peering over Mark's shoulder at his homework, and noticed an easy mistake.

"Isn't eight times four thirty-two?" he'd innocently asked. "You wrote down thirty-four."

Mark stuck out his tongue and pushed so hard on his pencil that the lead broke.

"See what you made me do?" he complained. "If you're so smart, why don't you go to school for me?"

Mother was hovering over them.

"Hush," she said to Mark, and that had been the end of it.

Luke's family didn't dwell on what they all knew: Because Luke was the third born, he was illegal, violating the Population Law with every breath he took and every bite of food he ate. Of course he couldn't go to school, or anywhere else.

But here he was, now, at school. And it wasn't Matthew and Mark's little country school, but a grand, fancy place that only the richest people, Barons, could afford. Rich people like the real Lee Grant, who had died in a skiing accident. His family had concealed his death and secretly given his identity card to help a shadow child come out of hiding.

Couldn't everyone tell that Luke was an impostor?

Luke wished the real Lee Grant were still alive. He wished that he, himself, were still at home, hiding.

"Young man," someone said in a warning voice.

Luke glanced around. He was the only one still standing. Quickly he slipped into the nearest vacant chair. He didn't have any books to study or work to do. Maybe this was the time to read the note from Jen's dad.

But as he reached into his pocket he knew it wasn't safe. The boy across the table from him kept looking up, the boy two chairs down kept whispering and pointing. Though Luke kept his head down, he could feel eyes all around him. Even if no one was looking directly at him, Luke felt

MARGARET PETERSON HADDIX

itchy and anxious just being in the same room with so many other people. He couldn't read the note. He could barely keep himself from bolting out of his chair, running out the door, finding some closet or small space to hide in.

And then everybody would know that he wasn't really Lee Grant. Everybody would know that all he knew was how to hide.

Luke forced himself to sit still for two hours.

When a bell went off again, everyone trouped down a hall to a huge dining area.

Luke hadn't eaten since breakfast at home—his mother's lightest biscuits and, as a miraculous farewell treat, fresh eggs. Luke could remember the pride shining in her eyes as she had slid the plate in front of him.

"From the factory?" he had asked. Eggs usually were not available for ordinary people, but his mother worked at a chicken factory, and if her supervisors were in a good mood, sometimes she got extra food.

Mother had nodded. "I promised them forty hours of overtime in exchange. Unpaid."

Luke had gulped.

"Just for two eggs for me?"

Mother had looked at him.

"It was a good trade," she'd said.

Remembering breakfast gave him a lump in his throat as big as an egg. He wasn't hungry.

But he sat down, because all the other boys were sitting. Instantly another boy turned on him and glared.

"Seniors only," he said.

"Huh?" Luke asked.

"Only seniors are allowed at this table," the boy said, in the same kind of mocking voice that Mark always used with Luke when Luke had said something dumb.

"Oh," Luke said.

"What are you, some kind of a lecker?" another boy asked.

Luke didn't know how to answer that. He was so eager to get up, he tripped and crashed into the next table.

"Juniors only," a boy said there.

Luke tried to swallow the lump in his throat, but it had grown even bigger.

He went from table to table, not even bothering to try to sit down. At each table, someone said in a bored voice, "Sophomores only," or "Freshmen only," or "Eights only" . . . Luke didn't know what he was, so he kept moving.

Finally he reached an empty table and sat down.

A bowl of leaves and what looked like germinating soybeans sat in front of him. Was this supposed to be food? The other boys were eating it, so he did, too. The leaves were clammy and bitter and stuck in his throat.

Luke let himself think about potato chips. Nobody was supposed to have junk food, because of the food shortages that led to the Population Law. But Jen had given him potato chips when he'd gone over to her house, secretly, at great risk. He could still taste the salt, could still feel the crisp chips against the roof of his mouth, could still hear

Jen saying, when he protested that potato chips were illegal, "Yeah, well, we're illegal, too, so why don't we enjoy ourselves?"

Jen. If Jen were here now, she wouldn't put up with bitter leaves and tasteless bean sprouts for supper. She'd be standing up, demanding decent food. She'd go to any table she wanted. She'd march up to the person in charge—the headmaster?—and say, "Why won't anyone tell me what classes to go to? What are demerits? What are the rules, anyway? You're not running this school very well!" She'd punch Rolly right in the eye.

But Jen wasn't there. Jen was dead.

Luke bent his head low over his food. He stopped even pretending to chew and swallow.

After supper everyone was herded into another vast room. A man stood at the front talking about how glorious the Government was, about how their leaders' wisdom had kept them all from starving.

Lies, Luke thought, and marveled that he had the will even to think that.

Finally another bell rang and the other boys scattered. Luke walked uncertainly up and down strange halls.

"To your room," a man warned him. "Lights out in ten minutes."

Luke was so eager to get to his room, he actually found his voice.

"I-I'm new. I don't know where my room is."

"Well, then, find out."

"How?" Luke asked.

The man sighed, and rolled his eyes.

"What's your name?" he asked, slowly, as though Luke might be too stupid to understand the question.

"L—" Somehow Luke couldn't bring himself to claim his fake identity. "I know my room number. One fifty-six. I just don't remember where it is."

"Why didn't you say so?" the man growled. "Up those stairs and around the corner."

Even with the man's directions, Luke got turned around and had to search and search. By the time he finally saw the engraved 156, his legs were trembling with exhaustion and his feet were blistered from walking in the stiff, unfamiliar shoes. Luke was used to going barefoot. He was used to sitting in the house all day, not walking up and down stairs and through labyrinth-like halls.

He stepped through the doorway and headed straight for his bed. It had a spread on it and looked like all the others now. All Luke wanted to do was fall into it and go to sleep and forget everything that had happened that day.

"Did you ask permission?" someone barked at him.

Luke looked around. He was so tired, he hadn't even noticed that seven boys were sitting on the floor in a circle, playing some sort of card game.

"Per-Permission?" he asked.

One of the boys—probably the one who'd spoken— threw back his head and laughed. He was tall and thin, and older than Luke. Maybe even as old as Luke's brother

MARGARET PETERSON HADDIX

Matthew, who was fifteen. But Matthew was familiar, known. Luke couldn't read this boy's expression. He had a strange cast to his dark eyes, and his face was oddly shaped. Something about him reminded Luke of the pictures he'd seen in books of jackals.

"Hey!" the boy said. "They sent us a voice replicator. Amazingly human-like form. Voice is a little off, though. Let's try another one. Repeat after me: 'I am an exnay. I am a fonrol. I am a lecker. I don't deserve to live.'"

Most of the other boys were laughing now, too, but quietly, as if they didn't want to miss Luke's answer.

Luke hesitated. He'd heard those words before: Rolly had called him an exnay and a fonrol, and someone had called him a lecker at dinner. Maybe they were from that foreign language the short, fat teacher had been speaking. Luke had no idea what the words meant, but he could tell that they were probably bad things. Thanks to Matthew and Mark, he could spot a setup.

Luke shook his head.

The jackal boy sighed in exaggerated disappointment.

"Broken already," he said. He stood up and knocked his fist against Luke's side the way Luke had seen his father tap on the engine of broken tractors or trucks. "You just can't get good junk nowadays."

Luke pulled away. He stepped toward his bed.

Jackal boy laughed again.

"Oh, no, not so fast. Permission, remember? Say, 'I am your servant, O mighty master. I shall do your bidding forever. I will not eat or sleep or breathe unless you say it is to be so.'"

The boy moved between Luke and his bed. The others leaned forward, menacingly. *Like a pack of jackals,* Luke thought.

Jackals were nasty, vicious animals. Luke had read a book about them. They tore their prey limb from limb sometimes.

These were really boys, not jackals, Luke reminded himself. But he was too tired to fight.

"I am your servant," he mumbled. "I—I don't remember the rest."

"Why do they always send us the stupid ones?" the jackal boy asked. He looked down at Luke. "Bet you don't even know your own name."

"L-Lee," Luke whispered, looking down at his shoes.

"Lee, repeat after me. 'I—'"

"I—"

"'Am—'"

"Am—"

The jackal boy fed him each word and Luke, hating himself, repeated it. Then the boy made him touch his elbow to his nose. Cross his eyes. Stand on one foot while reciting, "I am the lowest of the low. Everyone should spit on me," five times. The lights flickered and went out in the middle of this ordeal, and still the jackal boy continued. Finally he yawned. Luke could hear his jaw crack in the dark.

"New boy, you bore me," he said. "Remove yourself from my presence."

"Huh?" Luke said.

"Go to bed!"

Meekly, Luke slipped beneath his covers. He was still wearing his clothes—even his shoes—but he didn't dare get back up to take them off. The unfamiliar pants bunched up around his waist, and he silently smoothed them out. Touching his pocket reminded him: He still hadn't read the note from Jen's dad.

Tomorrow, Luke thought. He felt a little bit of hope return. Tomorrow he would read the note, and then he would know how to find out what classes to go to, how to deal with boys like Rolly and his roommates, how to get by. No—not just to get by. Luke remembered what he'd hoped for, leaving home—was it only that morning? It seemed so long ago. He'd been thinking about making a difference in the world, finding some way to help other third children who had to hide. Luke didn't expect the note from Jen's dad to tell him how to do that, but it would give him a start. It would make that possible.

All he had to do was go to sleep and then it would be tomorrow and he could read the note.

But Luke couldn't sleep. The room was filled with unfamiliar sounds: first the other boys whispering, then breathing deeply, in sleep. The beds creaking when someone turned over. Some vent somewhere blowing air on them all.

Luke ached, missing his room at home, his family, Jen.

And his own name. He felt his lips draw together.

"Luke," he whispered soundlessly, in the dark. "My name is Luke."

He waited silently, his heart pounding, but nothing happened. No alarm bells went off, no Population Police swooped in to carry him away. His feeling of hope surged, even more than the fear. His name was Luke. He was nobody's servant. He was not the lowest of the low. He was Dad and Mother's son. He was Matthew and Mark's brother. He was Jen's friend.

Or—he had been.

MARGARET PETERSON HADDIX

CHAPTER *FIVE*

uke didn't get a chance to read the note from Jen's dad the next day. Or the next. Or the next.

In fact, an entire week went by with him resolving every night in bed, "Tomorrow. Surely I'll find a way to read the note tomorrow." But the next nightfall found him still stymied.

At first, he thought there was an easy solution. The bathroom, for example. He could go in, shut the door, read the note.

But none of the bathrooms at Hendricks were like the bathroom at home, closed-in and private. The Hendricks bathrooms were rows of urinals and commodes, right out in front of everyone. Even the shower was communal, just an open, tiled room with dozens of spigots sprouting from each wall.

Luke could barely bring himself to lower his pants with everyone watching, let alone read the note. He always lingered until most of the other boys were gone, but he never found a bathroom that fully emptied out. Finally, after three days had passed and he was getting desperate, he resolved to wait in the bathroom for as long as it took, regardless of bells or classes. The bell rang for breakfast and still he remained, pretending to be very concerned with scrubbing his face.

Finally it was just Luke and another boy, standing by the door.

"Out," the boy said.

The boy was mean-faced and muscular. Luke's legs trembled, but he didn't shut off the water.

"I'm not done," Luke mumbled, trying to sound nonchalant, unconcerned. He failed miserably.

The boy grabbed Luke's arm.

"Didn't you hear me? I said OUT!" The boy jerked so hard on Luke's arm that Luke felt pain shoot through his whole body. Then the boy shoved Luke out the door. Luke landed in a heap on the hallway floor. A hall monitor looked down at him in disgust.

"You're late for breakfast," he said. "Two demerits."

Luke feebly looked from the hall monitor to the other boy, who was now standing menacingly in the bathroom doorway. Then he understood: They were alike. There were guards in all the bathrooms, as well as in all the halls. He couldn't read the note in either place.

He wondered about trying to read the note in his room. He would get there first at bedtime, he decided. The first several days this was impossible because, no matter how hard he tried, he couldn't ever remember which way to go. Left at the top of the stairs, then right, then right, then left? Or was it right, then left, then left, then right? Most nights, it was a miracle if he found the room at all before lights out. Though that was just as well, because it reduced the amount of time that jackal boy could spend tormenting him.

MARGARET PETERSON HADDIX

Finally, in the middle of Luke's second week at Hendricks, he sat at the back of the hall during the evening lecture, so he was the first one up the stairs. Holding his breath, he counted off the turns. Right—yes. Right—yes. Left. And there—yes! Room 156.

Luke rushed in past the hall monitor. He slipped behind the door, out of sight, and jammed his hand in his pocket. And heard, "So my servant's reporting for duty early tonight, eh?"

It was jackal boy, lounging on his bed.

Luke had to bite his lip to keep from screaming.

That night jackal boy was crueler than ever.

Luke had to repeat, "I am a fonrol," fifty times. He had to hop up and down on one foot for five minutes. He had to do one hundred push-ups. (He'd never seen anyone do a push-up before. All the other boys howled with laughter when he stammeringly confessed, "I—I don't know how.") He had to push a marble across the floor with his nose.

Lying in bed that night, Luke despaired. His shoulders ached from the push-ups; his side was still bruised from being thrown out of the bathroom.

I'll never get to read the note, he thought. *I'll never be alone.*

It wasn't just that he wanted to read the note. It was maddening to always be around other people, to know that his every action might be observed, to never have a second of privacy.

How could he long to be alone, and feel so lonely, all at once?

CHAPTER SIX

L uke got by.

It wasn't really that hard, as long as he didn't let himself want anything.

As long as he didn't linger in the bathroom or halls, as long as he sat down promptly when he entered a classroom, as long as he didn't try to eat at the wrong table, nobody bothered him except jackal boy. And jackal boy's torture was bearable, even at its worst.

The problem was, Luke couldn't always stop himself from wanting more.

He wanted home and he wanted his family and he wanted Jen alive again. And he wanted all the third children to be free, so he didn't have to go around pretending to be someone else anymore.

Those were impossible dreams, little fantasies that he played with in his mind in the middle of the night when he couldn't sleep.

The glow of those fantasies always made reality seem even bleaker the next morning.

But everything else he wanted seemed impossible, too.

MARGARET PETERSON HADDIX

He wanted to be able to climb into bed each night without even looking at jackal boy—without saying, "I am the
dumbest lecker alive," a hundred times, without doing a
single push-up, pull-up, sit-up, or toe-touch. Once during
a nightly session, he dared to mumble, "Leave me alone," to
jackal boy. But when Luke looked up, jackal boy was laughing hysterically.

"Did you—did you say what I thought—you said?" he
sputtered between laughs. "'Leave me alone.' Oh, that's a
good one, you stupid fonrol. You going to make me? Go
ahead. Make me."

Jackal boy had his fists up, a taunting grin smeared
across his face. Behind him, their other roommates gathered, eager for a fight. Eager, it seemed, to help jackal boy
pound every shred of courage out of Luke.

Luke sized up the height and weight difference just
between him and jackal boy. Never mind the rest of the
boys. Nobody had to swing a single punch. Luke's courage
was already gone.

At least jackal boy tortured Luke only once a day.

Three times a day, in the cavernous dining hall, Luke
longed for food that tasted good. Mouthing bitter greens
and mealy bread, he dreamed of Mother's stews, her biscuits, her apple pies. He could remember the exact sound
of her voice asking him, "Want to lick the bowl?" whenever she made a cake. And then the taste of sweet batter.

He could remember every detail of the one time that he
and Jen had made cookies together. They'd used special

chips made of chocolate, and when the cookies were done and hot from the oven, the chips were melted and sweet on his tongue. He and Jen sat in the kitchen laughing and talking and eating cookie after cookie after cookie.

That was one of the best visits he'd ever had with Jen.

It was also one of the last.

He tried to forget that, but he couldn't. He knew that if he sat down in the Hendricks dining hall and someone put a whole plateful of the Jen cookies in front of him, they'd taste every bit as bitter as the greens. He wouldn't be able to eat a bite.

And Mother's biscuits, flown in fresh—if that were possible—would crumble in his mouth just like the mealy bread. Nothing could taste good when you ate alone in the midst of hundreds of boys who didn't even know your name. Who didn't care.

For Luke wanted a friend at Hendricks, too. Sometimes he forced himself to stop daydreaming and start paying attention to the other boys. He wasn't brave enough to speak to any of them, but he thought if he listened, then someday . . .

He couldn't tell the boys apart.

Maybe it had something to do with being in hiding all those years. He wasn't blind—he could tell that some of them had different-colored hair, even slightly different-colored skin. Some were taller, some were shorter; some were fatter, some were thinner. Some of them were older even than Luke's brothers; others were a few years younger than Luke himself. But Luke could never fix any of them in his mind. Even jackal boy was unrecognizable outside of their room. Once he came up to Luke and said, "Ah, my servant! Just when I need a pen. Give me yours, kid." And Luke stared, openmouthed, for so long that jackal boy just eased the pen out of Luke's hand and headed off, muttering, "Fine time to turn statue on me."

Another time, during breakfast, he overheard boys joking at a nearby table.

"Oh, come on, Spence," one boy said to another.

Luke stared. *Spence,* he repeated to himself, memorizing the boy's features. *That boy's name is Spence. Now I know who he is.* It gave him a warm glow all morning, to think that he'd be able to recognize somebody now.

At lunch he watched Spence slip into his seat. Luke practically smiled. Then Spence knocked over his water glass, dousing the boy beside him.

"Ted, you lecker!" the other boy exclaimed.

Ted? But—

At dinner, the boy Luke would have sworn was Spence looked up when someone called out, "Hey! E. J.!"

"Not now," Spence/Ted/E. J. said irritably. Or was he simply E. J., and Spence and Ted were totally different boys?

Luke gave up trying to keep track of anybody's names. He thought he noticed other boys responding to multiple names, too, but he could never be sure.

Why was he so easily confused?

It was like the halls of the school, which always seemed to double back on themselves. From one day to the next, Luke could rarely find his way to the same classroom twice. So it didn't matter that he was never sure which class he was supposed to be sitting in—he'd never be able to get to the right place, anyhow. The teachers didn't seem to notice Luke, or anyone else. They'd occasionally point at a boy and declare, "Two demerits," but they almost never called anyone by name.

Luke wondered about sneaking up to his room during classtime, and reading the note from Jen's dad, since nobody cared where he was, anyway. But the hall monitors guarded the stairs, too. They guarded everything.

So, Luke reflected gloomily, the note that could save him was doomed to turn to lint in his pocket. And Luke was doomed to endlessly wander the halls of Hendricks, unnoticed, unknowing, unknown.

In bed at night, Luke took to having imaginary conversations with his family, Jen, Jen's dad. His part was all apologies.

I'm sorry, Mr. Talbot. You risked your life to get me a fake I.D., and I wasn't worth it. . . .

I'm sorry, Jen, I'm not doing anything for the cause. . . .

I'm sorry, Mother. This was the hardest one of all. *You wanted me to stay but I said I had to go. I said I was going to make a difference in the world. But I can't. I wanted to make sure there was enough food for everyone in the world, so third children could be legal again. But I can't even understand a word my teachers say. Even the ones who are speaking my language. I'll never learn anything. I'll never be able to help anyone.*

I'm sorry, Mother. I should have never left you. I wish—

But Luke wished for so much, he couldn't go on.

He was so busy longing for big, impossible changes, he never gave a thought to wanting anything smaller or more practical. Like an open door.

But that was what he got.

CHAPTER *SEVEN*

Luke saw the door one morning on the way to class. He'd barely slept the night before, so he was groggy and stupid. He was shuffling along looking for a familiar classroom to duck into before the hall monitor yelled at him. Between classrooms, he stared down at his feet. too miserable to lift his head. But just as he turned a corner, someone bumped into him. Luke looked up in time to see the other boy barrel past without an apology. Then, as Luke turned his head forward again, he saw it.

The door was on the outside wall. Luke couldn't have said if he'd passed it a hundred times before, or never. It was solid wood with a brass knob, just like dozens of other doors in the school. It was barely even ajar.

But beyond it, Luke could see grass and trees and sky. Outdoors.

He didn't think. He didn't even pause to make sure a hall monitor wasn't watching him. In a flash, Luke was out the door.

Outside, Luke stood still, his back to the wall of the school. He was breathing hard. *Read the note and get back*

M ARGARET   P ETERSON   H ADDIX

inside! some tiny, rational part of his brain urged him. *Before someone sees you!*

But he couldn't move. It was May. The lawn ahead of him was a rich green carpet. Redbuds were blooming, and lilacs. He thought he even smelled honeysuckle. His mind played a trick on him, and suddenly he was almost a whole year back in time, standing outside for what he had thought might be the last time in his entire life. The Government workers were just starting to cut down the woods behind his family's house, and his mother was fearfully ordering him, "Luke! Inside. Now."

And when the woods were gone, Jen's house replaced it.

His mind skipped ahead, and he remembered his first trip to Jen's house. He'd stepped outside and felt paralyzed, just like now. And he'd marveled at the feel of fresh air on his face, just like now.

And he'd been in danger.

Just like now.

Luke looked back at the school, hopelessly. Anyone could easily look out a window and see him, and report him. Maybe they'd just give him more of those meaningless demerits. Or maybe this would make them realize that he really wasn't Lee Grant, that his papers were forged, that by the laws of the land, he deserved to die.

Strangely, Luke could see no windows. But the door was opening.

Luke took off running. He raced as blindly as he had that first day, trying to keep up with Rolly Sturgeon. Luke was crashing through the undergrowth of a small woods before his mind fully registered that there was a woods. Brambles tore at his arms and legs and chest, and he kept running. He whipped willow branches out of his way. He was so frenzied, he felt like he could run forever.

Then he tripped over a log and fell.

Silence. Only now that he'd stopped did Luke realize how much noise he'd been making. So stupid. Luke lay facedown in ferns and moss, and waited for someone to grab him and yell and punish him.

Nothing happened. Over the pounding of his pulse, Luke could hear nothing but birdsong. After what seemed like a very long time, he cautiously raised his head.

Trees formed a canopy over his head. A flash of movement caught Luke's eye, but it was only a squirrel jumping from branch to branch. Branches swayed, but only because of the wind.

Slowly, Luke inched back the way he had come. Finally he crouched, hidden by the underbrush, and spied on the school.

Nobody was in sight.

Luke peered at the door. It moved out again, and he stiffened, terrified. But then it moved in.

In, out, in, out—so slow—it was like the school was breathing through the door. Suddenly Luke understood.

Nobody had pushed the door open. It was the wind, or maybe the change in air pressure as the boys walked past.

Luke stuck his head out a little further. He could see one whole side of the school building this way. And he realized for the first time: There were no windows in any part of the wall. It was solid brick, up and down.

How could that be?

Luke thought about all of the rooms he'd been in, since coming to Hendricks, and it was true—he couldn't remember a single window in any of them. Even the room he shared with jackal boy and his minions was window-less. Why hadn't he ever noticed before?

And why would someone build so many windowless rooms?

Suddenly Luke didn't care. There were no windows, nobody was coming out of the door—he was safe.

"I can read the note now!" he said aloud, and chuckled. It was strangely thrilling to hear his own voice—not timid, not stammering—Luke's voice, not the pretend-Lee's.

"I'm going to read it right over there!" he said, speaking just for the pleasure of it. "Finally!"

He strolled deeper into the woods, and sat down on the very log he'd tripped over before. Slowly, ceremoniously, he slipped the note from Jen's dad out of his pocket. Now he would know everything he needed to do.

He unfolded the note, which had grown worn from all the times he'd palmed it, secretly transferring it from the pocket of one pair of pants to another. Then he stared, try-ing to make sense of Mr. Talbot's scrawl.

The note only held two words:

Blend in

CHAPTER *EIGHT*

"**N**o!" Luke screamed.

That was it? "Blend in"? What kind of advice was that? Luke needed help. He'd been waiting weeks.

"I was counting on you!" Luke screamed again, past caring who might hear.

The "B" on "Blend" blurred before his eyes. Desperately, he turned the note over, hoping there was more on the other side. The real message, maybe. But the other side was blank. What he held was just a small, ragged scrap of paper, not much more than lint. Even Mother—who saved everything, who reused envelopes—even she wouldn't think twice about tossing this useless shred in the trash.

And this tiny piece of nothing was what Luke had pinned all his hopes on.

Too furious to see straight, Luke ripped the note in half. In fourths. In eighths. He kept ripping until the pieces of paper were all but dust. Practically microscopic. Then he threw them as far away as he could.

"I hate you, Mr. Talbot!" Luke yelled.

The words echoed in the trees. Even the woods seemed

to be making fun of him. That was probably all Mr. Talbot had meant to do, too, when he'd handed Luke the note that first day. Luke could just imagine Mr. Talbot chuckling as he drove away from Hendricks after leaving Luke. He probably thought it was funny to drop off a dumb farm boy at a snobby Baron school and tell him, "Blend in." He probably laughed about it all the time. If Jen were still alive, she probably would have laughed at Luke, too.

No. Not Jen . . .

Luke buried his face in his hands and slipped down to the ground, sprawled beside the log. Without the note to count on, he didn't even have enough backbone of his own to sit.

CHAPTER *NINE*

Luke wouldn't have thought he could have fallen asleep there in the woods, in danger, boiling mad. But somehow he found himself waking up some time later, stiff and sore and confused. The birds were still singing, a mild breeze ruffled his hair—before he remembered everything, Luke actually smiled. What a pleasant dream. But why did he feel so unhappy?

Then he sat up and opened his eyes and everything came back to him. The note he'd believed in so fervently was worthless dust now—no matter how hard he peered off into the underbrush, he couldn't see a single sign of it. He was out in the woods, violating who knew how many rules of the Hendricks School for Boys. And he had no idea how long he'd been gone—squinting at the sun, Luke guessed that it was at least mid-afternoon. They must have noticed him missing by now. He should be thinking up his excuse now. He should sneak back so at least they wouldn't find him out here. It wouldn't look so bad. Maybe he could convince them that he'd started to run away—the real Lee Grant had done that, supposedly—then repented and turned around. But that story depended on him going back *now*.

Luke didn't move.

He didn't want to go back to school. Not now, not ever. There wasn't anything there for him. He knew that now. No friends, no helpful teachers, no good choices. He was just like some windup toy there, marching mindlessly from class to class, meal to meal, trying not to be watched.

Just the thought of school made his stomach churn.

"You can't make me go back," Luke muttered, though he wasn't sure who he thought he was defying.

That was settled. So where else could he go?

Home . . .

Luke was overcome with a stronger longing than he'd ever felt before. To see Mother again, to see Dad . . . This was how miserable Luke felt: He even missed his brothers. He watched a chipmunk race across the ground. The chipmunk's feet barely seemed to touch. It could be just that easy for Luke, going home. All he had to do was start walking.

But.

He didn't know how to get there. Even if he had a map, he wouldn't be able to find his parents' farm on it.

He didn't have his fake I.D. card with him. He didn't carry it at school. He could picture it clearly, tucked in the pocket at the back of his suitcase. He couldn't go back for it. And getting caught without an I.D. card was as good as admitting, "I'm a third child. Kill me."

Luke tried to pretend those weren't obstacles. He still couldn't picture a perfect homecoming.

Even if he managed to find his family's farm without running into the Population Police first, he'd just be bringing danger with him. The penalties for harboring an illegal child were almost as harsh as the penalty for *being* an illegal child. Every second he'd lived with his parents, he'd put their lives in jeopardy. And now there was a record of his existence. If he disappeared now, someone would have to look for him. And when they found him, cowering in his family's attic, they'd be sure to find out the truth as well.

Luke picked up a pebble and threw it far into the woods. It wasn't fair. His only choices were to be miserable at school or a virtual murderer at home. He threw another pebble, and another. Not fair, not fair, not fair. He ran out of pebbles and switched to bark chips, peeled off the log beside him. Some of the pebbles and bark chips hit tree trunks with a satisfying thud. Luke began aiming.

"Take that!" he yelled, forgetting himself.

Then, terrified, he clapped his hand over his mouth. How could he be so stupid?

He froze, listening so hard, his ears began to buzz. But there was no sound of anyone tramping through the woods looking for him. There was no sound from the school at all. Peering around at the ferns and the trees and the sunlight filtering through the branches, Luke could practically convince himself the school didn't exist at all.

It was a shame he couldn't just stay here.

Luke had a moment of hope—he could live on nuts and berries. He could hide in the trees whenever they came looking for him.

But that was a childish plan. He dismissed it immediately. If he stayed in the woods, he'd be caught or starve.

He glanced around again, this time regretfully. The trees looked friendlier than any of the boys or teachers at schools. He was a farm boy who'd spent most of his life outdoors, until the woods were cut down behind his house. Just being outside was a joy. And no matter how much he'd risked, running out here, it was wonderful to be alone, not packed in and watched at every turn.

Luke dug the toe of his fancy Baron shoe into the dirt and stood up. He'd come to a decision without realizing it. He had to go back to school. He owed it to his family, and Jen's dad, and maybe even Jen herself.

But nothing could stop him from visiting the woods again.

CHAPTER TEN

L uke put off returning to school as long as possible. His stomach growled and he ignored it. The angle of the sun's rays grew sharper and sharper, but he consoled himself, "It's still daylight. It just starts looking like twilight sooner, when you're deep in the woods."

Finally he could ignore the truth no longer. It was getting dark. And even if nobody had noticed his absence so far, he'd be missed at bedtime. Jackal boy was sure to complain if Luke wasn't there for him to pick on.

Strangely, that thought almost made him feel good.

Luke didn't stop to figure that one out. He strode to the edge of the woods, looked around carefully, then took off running across the lawn.

Halfway to the school, he was struck by a horrible thought: What if the door was locked?

A few steps later, he was close enough to tell: The door wasn't open anymore. It wasn't even ajar.

Luke dashed even faster across the lawn, as if he could outrun his panic. His heart pounded, and it wasn't just from running. He'd been so stupid, going out the door in the first place. Or, if he'd had to step outside, why hadn't he gone back right away? Why had he risked everything for a day in the woods?

He knew why.

Luke was finally close enough to touch the doorknob. He reached out with a trembling hand, prepared for the worst.

Stay calm, stay calm, he told himself. *If it's locked, maybe you can find another door that works. Maybe you can still slip back in undetected. Maybe . . .* Luke didn't have much faith in "maybes."

Hopelessly, he twisted the knob.

The knob turned easily.

Barely daring to believe his luck, Luke pulled the door open a crack. He couldn't see anyone, so he slid in and let the door close behind him. It was dark at this end of the hall. He appreciated the shadows.

Luke was tiptoeing past vacant classrooms when he heard the shout.

"Hey! What are you doing down here?"

It was one of the hall monitors.

"I—I got lost," Luke said, not stammering any more than he would have under normal circumstances. And the excuse was entirely plausible—hadn't he been lost a million times so far at school? But he didn't know what he was missing. Supper? The evening lecture? Lights out?

The hall monitor peered at him suspiciously.

"Nobody's supposed to be in this wing of the building

right now," he said. "Why did you leave the dining hall?"

Luke got a sudden inspiration.

"I got sick," he said. "I ran out to go to the bathroom. Then I got lost when I was going back."

The hall monitor looked skeptical.

"The bathroom's right across from the dining hall," he said.

"I—I wasn't paying attention. I'm new. I was sick." Luke tried to look dumb enough—and queasy enough—to have made such a stupid mistake.

The hall monitor took a step back, like he didn't want to catch anything.

"Okay," he relented. "Go back immediately."

Relieved, Luke turned to go. Then he stopped. Only the day before, he would have obeyed unthinkingly. But now he had a secret to protect. Now he had to be crafty. He turned back to the monitor.

"I don't know how to get there. Remember?"

"Oh, for crying out loud. Why do I have to baby-sit all the leckers?" He took Luke's arm and jerked him to the right. "Go that way. Turn left at the first hallway, then left and right again. Just get out of here!"

The hall monitor sounded a little panicked himself. The day before, Luke wouldn't have noticed, but now he had to pay attention. *Something about that door*, Luke thought. *Why is the hall monitor so desperate to get me away from it?*

Luke was still pondering that question when he reached the doors to the dining hall. They burst open, and boys streamed out. Luke's timing was perfect: He'd gotten there just as everyone was heading toward the evening lecture. He blended in. *See, Mr. Talbot?* he thought bitterly. *I am following the only bit of advice you saw fit to give me. Aren't you proud? Mighty generous of you, I'm sure.*

But some of Luke's bitterness had eased. The note had been worthless, but he had the woods to think about now. And if the note had led him to the woods—well, he did have reason to be grateful to Jen's dad, didn't he?

Nobody challenged Luke as he walked into the lecture room and sat down. Nobody asked, "Where have you been all day?" Nobody ordered him, "Never leave this building again!"

He'd gotten away with it. He could get away with it again.

CHAPTER ELEVEN

L uke longed to race straight to the woods as soon as
he woke up the next morning. It was torture to stand
patiently beside all the other boys, splashing water on his
face. It was torture to sit still and slowly spoon in the
lumpy oatmeal, when he longed to gulp it down and get
out of there. (Though, since he'd missed two meals the day
before, it was amazing how delicious the oatmeal seemed
for once.) It was torture waiting for the cafeteria doors to
open and release everyone else to classes, and Luke to the
woods.

As soon as breakfast was over, he took off, all but running. Surprisingly, given how confused he usually got in
the Hendricks halls, he managed to make a beeline straight
for the door, without once making a wrong turn and having to retrace his steps. Approaching the door, he slowed
down, waiting for the crowd to clear in the hall. Finally,
there was only Luke and a hall monitor, several yards away.
The door wasn't open today, but Luke was confident that it
wasn't locked. He was confident that he could slip out
quickly enough. He glanced back. The monitor was looking

the other way. Now! Luke reached for the doorknob—

—and then drew back.

At the last minute, it was like someone or something screamed, *"No!"* in his mind. Mother had talked about God sometimes—maybe that's who it was. Or maybe it was Jen's spirit, come to help Luke when her father's note hadn't. Maybe it was just Luke's own common sense. Luke didn't know what he thought about God or ghosts or even his own intelligence, but he knew: He couldn't risk going to the woods today.

Luke walked on, pretending to be casually dawdling.

"Get to class," the monitor growled.

Luke nodded, and stepped into the next classroom he passed. He felt as disappointed as if he'd discovered bars on the door. What was he—a coward?

Luke remembered all the mind games he'd played with himself trying to get up the nerve to go to Jen's house that first time. He'd waited weeks, always telling himself he was just waiting for the right moment. He had been a coward then.

But he wasn't being a coward now. Sinking into a seat, as anonymous as every other boy in the room, he actually felt brave, clever, crafty.

Probably he'd just gotten lucky the day before. If he wanted to be able to go the woods again and again and again, without getting caught, he'd have to be smart about it. He'd have to pay attention to everything. Maybe he'd even have to figure out why the hall monitor the night before had been so panicky. Before he went back again, he'd have to know it was safe.

Luke looked around the room. Up front, the teacher was drawing complicated-looking mathematical formulas on the chalkboard. Luke couldn't have solved any of them if his life depended on it. But for once, instead of sinking into despair and staring down at the desk in front of him, Luke got the nerve to peer around at the other boys. A few were watching the teacher. A few were taking notes—er, no, they were drawing pictures of naked girls. Some were blatantly sleeping, their mouths slack-jawed. And some were sitting off to the side, their arms clutched around their legs, rocking.

Luke stared. He didn't have much to go on, since he'd only known six people before in his entire life, but that rocking certainly didn't seem like normal behavior.

Eventually the bell rang, and he stumbled into another class. It was the same there: some boys acting normal, some boys rocking endlessly.

Why hadn't he noticed anything like that before?

He knew why. Every other time he'd looked directly at any of the other boys, he'd glanced quickly, then looked away, for fear that they might actually look back.

You could miss a lot, doing that.

Walking through the hall to his next class, Luke tried an experiment: He stared directly into the eyes of every single boy who went past him.

It was terrifying—even worse than running blindly

across a lawn. Luke's stomach seized up, and he thought he might actually throw up his breakfast oatmeal. He thought his legs might crumple under him, in fear.

But it was also interesting.

Most of the other boys he passed looked away as soon as Luke made eye contact. Some of them seemed to have a sort of sixth sense that warned them off from letting Luke look at them in the first place. Only two or three stared boldly back, their eyes locked on Luke's just as Luke's were locked on theirs.

Remember them, Luke ordered himself. But it took all his willpower just to keep himself from looking away.

When he finally arrived in a classroom doorway, Luke was shaking all over.

I gave something away, just then, he thought. *Now they'll know.*

But he didn't know who "they" were.

CHAPTER *TWELVE*

Luke made himself wait an entire week before he went back to the woods. But in that time, no matter how closely he paid attention to everything, the mysteries only seemed to multiply.

For example, by the end of the week, Luke was even more baffled by the lack of windows than ever before. Because he'd discovered: There wasn't a single window in the entire place.

To learn that, Luke had to make himself figure out the floor plan of the entire school. He had to be sure that he peeked into every classroom, every sleeping room, every office. One morning at breakfast, he even pretended to get turned around and plowed straight into the kitchen. Two cooks screamed, and Luke was given a stern lecture and a record ten demerits, but he found out what he wanted to know: Even the kitchen lacked windows.

Why? Why would anyone build a windowless school?

Luke wondered if there'd been something unusual about his family's house, that it had had windows, and he'd just accepted it as the norm. But, no—all the houses and schools and other buildings Luke had seen in books had had windows. And when the Government built Jen's neighborhood, all the houses there had windows. And Jen's family and their neighbors were Barons—if Baron houses had windows, why didn't Baron schools?

Luke couldn't figure out the other boys, either. There were rocking boys in most of his classes, he realized now. Several times, Luke practically hypnotized himself staring at them. But they seemed harmless enough.

The boys who worried Luke were the ones he called "the starers"—the ones who looked back when he looked at them.

All the hall monitors were starers.

So was jackal boy.

Luke tried to tell himself that the starers bothered him only because he'd spent so much time in hiding. Of course he didn't like being stared at. They were probably just act-ing normal, and he was in danger of giving away his real identity by getting disturbed by it.

Somehow he couldn't believe that.

At night when jackal boy tormented him, Luke kept his eyes trained carefully on the ground. But he could feel jackal boy's gaze on the side of his face as definitely as he would feel a slap or a punch.

"Say, 'I am an exnay of the worst order,'" jackal boy ordered him as usual one evening.

Luke mumbled the words. He wondered what would happen if he looked up and unleashed his questions on jackal boy: Why do you stare? Why aren't there any windows? Why do we never go outside? Why was the door open that one day? And finally: Are there any other shadow children here?

But of course he couldn't ask jackal boy. Jackal boy thought it was funny to make Luke wave his arms for five minutes straight. Jackal boy was only interested in humiliating Luke. He'd probably think it was amusing to tell the Population Police, "I know where you can find a third child. How big's my reward?"

So Luke bit his tongue and gritted his teeth and touched his finger to his nose fifty times, as ordered. He jogged in place until his legs ached. He reached for his toes again and again, until jackal boy said in a bored voice, "Get out of my sight."

Luke crawled into bed unsure whether to be relieved that he hadn't blown his cover, or disappointed that he hadn't found the answers to his questions.

That night in bed, he was too busy puzzling over all his mysteries to even think about whispering his own name. When he had his pretend conversations, he asked advice, instead of offering apologies.

What do you think, Jen? What's wrong with this place? Is there something wrong? You went out into the world on fake passes all the time. Do people everywhere act like the boys at Hendricks?

And, *Mother, Dad, what's your opinion? Is it okay if I go out into the woods again?*

But it was ridiculous to feel like he had to get permission from parents he'd never see again. Or to ask advice from a friend who was dead. It was just too bad that that was all he had.

Luke swallowed a lump in his throat. He couldn't solve the school's mysteries. But he was going back to the woods no matter what.

CHAPTER *THIRTEEN*

L uke worked out a plan for leaving the school every day after lunch, and coming back right before dinner. It was sort of a compromise—he thought he ought to go to some classes, no matter how little sense they made to him. And this way he wouldn't miss any meals. He was already hungry all the time. He already had trouble keeping his fancy Baron pants hitched up on his scrawny frame.

The first day he left, he slipped out while the hall monitor was looking the other way. He knew now that none of the other boys would even notice.

So easy, Luke thought to himself as he jogged across the lawn to the woods. *Why don't all the boys escape out here?*

He decided it wasn't worth troubling himself with unanswerable questions.

The sun was shining, and he could tell that even the leaves that had been curled up and tiny a week earlier were full grown and spread out now. High overhead, the arc of tree limbs in some parts of the woods blocked out the sky completely. *It's like a cave,* Luke thought. But that reminded him of hiding and cowering indoors. He moved out into a clearing, where grass struggled to grow through last fall's dead leaves. It looked like there were raspberry plants, too, mostly buried in tangled brush.

"Raspberries," Luke whispered, his mouth watering. Mother grew raspberries, back home, and every June she kept the whole family stuffed with raspberry pies and cakes and breads. She made raspberry jam, too, and spread it on their toast and spooned it into their cornmeal mush all year long.

Luke eagerly searched the branches in front of him— tasting a raspberry would be like visiting home, just for a minute. But there weren't any berries yet, only an occasional bud. And it was likely the weeds would choke out those buds before they matured.

Unless Luke cleared the brush around them.

It only took Luke ten or fifteen minutes to pull the weeds and give the raspberry plants room, but by the time he was done, he had a full-blown idea in his head.

He could grow a whole garden out here. Surely no one would mind, or even find out. In his imagination he saw neat rows of sweet corn, tomato plants, and peas. He could put strawberries and blueberries over at the side of the clearing, where they'd get some shade. He'd want beans, too. Squash wasn't practical, because it wasn't much good raw. But there was always cucumber and zucchini, cantaloupe and watermelon . . . Luke's stomach growled.

Then he remembered seeds. He didn't have any.

Luke's dream instantly withered. How stupid was he that he thought he could grow a garden without seeds? Luke could imagine how Matthew and Mark would make fun of him if they knew. Even Dad and Mother would have a hard time not laughing. Just a month away from home and he'd already forgotten what you needed for a garden.

Luke stared at the measly raspberry plants in disappointment. Then he could almost hear Mother's voice in his ears: *Make the best of what you've got.* How many times had he heard her say that?

Even one raspberry would be delicious.

And maybe he could find blueberry or strawberry plants somewhere in the woods, and transplant them.

And maybe he could get seeds from some of the food at school. The bean sprouts they were always feeding him, for example—could he plant those? He didn't know what kind of beans they would grow into, but even if they were soybeans, Jen had told him once that the Government thought those were edible. Roasted, maybe. He could build a fire.

And maybe later in the summer, they would serve tomatoes or cantaloupe or watermelon, and he could smuggle the seeds to his room somehow. It would be too late for planting by then, but he could save the seeds for next year. . . .

It made Luke's throat ache to think of staying at Hendricks School a whole year. A whole year without his family, a whole year of grieving for Jen, a whole year of not speaking to anyone but jackal boy. A whole year of having nothing but a fake name and clothes that didn't fit.

Luke stood up and planted his feet firmly on the ground.

"I have the woods," he said aloud. "I'll have the garden. This is mine."

CHAPTER *FOURTEEN*

B y the end of the week, Luke had a nice plot of land cleared. The raspberry plants were at the center, and he had straight lines of bean sprouts planted on either side. It was Dad he pretended to appeal to most now.

"What do these look like to you, Dad?" he'd say aloud, as though Dad were really there to answer. "Am I just wasting my time? Or will I have a good crop come fall?"

Luke truly wasn't sure. But he felt so proud, looking at the neat little garden. He kept meaning to explore more of the woods, but he was always too busy digging and weeding, tending his plot. Anxiously he shooed away squirrels and chipmunks, and wished that he could stay out and guard his garden all the time.

But each afternoon he kept a close eye on the Baron watch he now wore on his wrist, so he could run back to the school promptly at six o'clock. He'd found the watch in his suitcase, and faced quite a chore figuring out how to read it. Those lines and "V's" and "X's" on it were numbers, he knew, but different from what he was used to. Why did Barons always have to make everything so fancy and com-

plicated? Back home Mother and Dad had just a single digital clock, in the kitchen. It blinked off the minutes ⹂s clear
as could be. This watch was like a foreign language to Luke.
But he stared at the angle of the rays of sun, he studied the
digital clocks at school and compared them with the watch
on his wrist—eventually he understood the Baron watch
as well as any other.

That made him feel proud, too.

So did his next accomplishment.

One day at lunch they served baked potatoes in the
school dining hall. They were so undercooked, they practically crunched. Luke bit into a raw end that hadn't even
had its eye removed. Spitting it out, he complained to
himself, *I'd rather plant this than eat it.*

Plant this. Of course. How many springs had Luke spent
cutting up potatoes for planting? He and Mother, perched
over a three-gallon bucket, knives flashing. When he was
little, he'd always tried to rest his feet on the top of the
bucket, the same way Mother did, but he was never tall
enough. Even when he was tall enough, he never balanced
things right. He'd tip the whole bucket over. Mother would
look at him sternly and sigh, "Pick it up." But then she'd
smile, like she wasn't really mad. She'd talk to him the whole
time they worked: "Careful with the knife—don't cut toward
your hand. You're making sure there's an eye in every
potato, aren't you? Nothing will grow without an eye."

But potatoes would grow without a seed. He just
needed a raw potato.

Covertly, Luke used his fork to separate the cooked and raw part of his potato. The raw part he dropped into his hand, and slipped into his pocket. Probably nobody had ever used Baron pants for transporting potato parts before, but Luke didn't care.

As soon as the bell rang for the end of lunch, Luke moved quickly among the tables, grabbing the left-behind potato pieces wherever he could. His pockets were stuffed in a matter of minutes.

He walked stiffly down the hall and out his door, trying not to smash the potatoes.

Nobody noticed.

Out in the woods, Luke dumped out his pockets and examined his treasure. He had eight potato pieces that looked like good candidates for planting. He wished he'd thought to smuggle a knife out of the dining hall, too, but that couldn't be helped. He halved as many of the potatoes as he could using his fingernails and brute force. Then he planted them in a row beside the beans.

When he was done, Luke sat back against a tree trunk and surveyed his work. It looked good. In a few days he'd know if anything was going to grow. He thought the bean sprouts looked bigger. At least they weren't withering yet.

After a few minutes of rest, Luke walked down to a creek that ran through the woods and cupped his hands in it, making trip after trip to bring back water for his garden. If only he had one of those three-gallon buckets now! Even a cup would help. Maybe he could bring one from the dining room.

In the meantime, he really didn't mind using his hands. Walking back and forth between the creek and his garden, Luke felt a strange surge of emotion, one he hadn't felt in so long that he'd practically forgotten what it was.

Happy, he thought in amazement. *I'm happy.*

CHAPTER *FIFTEEN*

The very next day Luke raced out to his garden even more eagerly than ever. It was too soon to tell anything about the potatoes, but if the beans still looked good, he could probably be sure that they would live and grow and produce. And would the raspberries have any more buds today?

Luke reached his clearing and stopped short.

His garden was destroyed.

The raspberry branches were broken off at odd angles; the bean plants were trampled, smashed flat in the mud. There hadn't been any potato shoots to be ruined, of course, but the garden was so messed up, Luke couldn't even tell where he'd planted them.

"No," Luke wailed. "It can't be."

He wanted to believe that he'd accidentally walked into the wrong clearing. But that was crazy. There was the maple tree with the jagged cut in its trunk on one side of the clearing, the oak with the sagging limb on the other side, the rotting trunk in the middle—this *was* his garden. Or—it had been.

Who wrecked it?

His first thought was animals. Back home, back when his family still raised hogs, there had been a couple of times when the hogs had escaped and found their way to the garden. They'd rooted around like crazy, and Mother had been furious over the damage.

But there weren't any hogs in the woods. Luke hadn't seen anything bigger than a squirrel. And for all his shooings and worrying, he knew squirrels couldn't have done this kind of damage.

And squirrels didn't wear shoes.

Luke winced. He'd been too distraught to notice before: Instead of animal tracks, the garden was covered with imprints of the same kind of shoes Luke was wearing. Smooth-soled Baron shoes had stomped on his raspberries, trampled his beans, kicked at his potato hills. They had walked all over his garden.

For a crazy instant, Luke wondered if he himself was to blame. Had he been careless leaving the garden yesterday? Could he have stepped on his own plants by mistake? That was ridiculous. He'd never do such a thing.

What if he'd sleepwalked, and come out here in the night without even knowing it?

That was even more preposterous. He would have been caught.

And he didn't wear shoes to bed.

Anyhow, he could tell by stepping next to the other footprints: Some of the imprints were made by shoes that were bigger than Luke's. Some of the imprints were made by shoes that were smaller.

Lots of people had been in Luke's garden. Lots of people had been there destroying it.

Luke sank to the ground by the tree trunk. He buried his face in his hands.

"This was all I had," he moaned. Once again he was pretending to talk to someone who wasn't there. But it wasn't Mother or Dad, Jen or Mr. Talbot he appealed to now. It was Matthew and Mark, his older brothers. He had to apologize to them. He had to explain why he, Luke Garner, a twelve-year-old boy, was crying.

CHAPTER *SIXTEEN*

L uke went back to school early that afternoon. What good would it do to stay in the garden? He'd only make himself more miserable. It wasn't worth trying to clean up, to replant. Whoever did this would only come back and destroy his garden again.

Washing his face in the creek before leaving, Luke tortured himself with questions. Who had done this? Who were the—vandals? The criminals? Luke couldn't even come up with a harsh enough word to describe them. Then he thought of the insults that had been hurled at him for the past month. Yes. The guilty ones were fonrols. Exnays. Leckers.

Luke wiped his face off on his sleeve, and it left a streak of mud. Who cared?

He circled wide leaving the creek so he didn't have to see his poor butchered garden again.

He didn't even bother running across the wide expanse of lawn back to the school. He trudged.

At the door, his brain woke again. He couldn't go back in now, in the middle of classes. He'd be noticed wandering the halls alone. How many people had yelled at him and

Rolly that first day? Luke looked at his watch and puzzled out the time. It was only one-thirty. It probably would be another half an hour before classes let out, and Luke could slip into the stream of other boys walking between rooms.

Luke leaned hopelessly against the rough brick wall beside the doorway. He almost welcomed the pain it brought, scraping his arm, pressing into his forehead. Maybe he should run back to the woods, where he could hide better, be safer. But he didn't care. He'd given up his name, his family—everything—for safety. Right now it didn't look like such a great deal.

Anyway, the woods didn't seem the least bit inviting anymore. They weren't his. They never had been.

Standing stoically before a closed door, Luke suddenly understood the clues he'd been too dense or blind—or hopeful—to notice before. Of course some of the other boys visited the woods. That's why the hall monitor had been so panicked that first night, when he saw Luke near the door. The monitor wasn't guarding the hall. He was guarding the door. Some boys had been planning to sneak out, that night, and the monitor was making sure it was safe. Probably they sneaked out to the woods all the time.

Luke could imagine how they'd acted, discovering the garden.

"Hey, look!" he could hear one boy calling to another. "Let's rip this up!"

And then they did—a horde of boys stomping the potatoes and yanking up the raspberries and hurling uprooted bean plants across the garden. Luke's garden.

"I'm going to find you," he whispered. "I'm going to get you."

CHAPTER *SEVENTEEN*

Promptly at two o'clock, Luke eased the door open a crack and peeked in. His timing was good—boys were walking to and from classes, their heads bowed, their eyes trained on the ground. But a hall monitor stood directly across from the door. Luke ducked back.

Look away, look away, Luke mentally commanded the monitor. Luke waited. Then, just when he moved over, ready to peek again, he saw the door slide shut.

Oh, no. Luke tried to figure out what had happened. Had the monitor seen the door open, thought that one of his marauding gang had forgotten to close it, and merely shut it to save his own skin?

Or did he know Luke was out there?

Stay calm, Luke commanded himself, uselessly. His panic boiled over. And his anger. He hated that monitor. He was probably one of the boys who'd trampled Luke's garden.

Luke could have looked for another door. He could have waited another hour, in hopes that a different hall monitor would be manning this spot, and not paying as much attention. He could have even gone back to the woods and waited until his usual time to come back.

But he didn't. He grabbed the doorknob and yanked.

As the door swung open, Luke saw that the hall monitor wasn't looking directly at the door just then. If Luke was sneaky enough, he could slip in without drawing attention to himself. But Luke let the door slam behind him. A cluster of boys with their eyes trained on the ground were jolted by the noise and even looked up briefly. Some of them started running, as panicked as if someone had fired a gun. Other boys didn't even glance Luke's way.

The hall monitor jerked his head around immediately. Luke quickly joined the slow-moving group of boys with their heads down. But just before he lowered his own head, Luke caught the hall monitor's stare. Their eyes locked for just an instant. Luke waited for the monitor to grab him by the collar, to yell, to haul him off to the headmaster's office. Luke could feel his shoulder hunching into a cower.

Nothing happened.

Luke shuffled forward with the other boys, and dared to look up again. The hall monitor was carefully looking past Luke.

He knows I was outside, Luke thought. *And he knows I know he knows. Why isn't he doing anything?*

It was like a chess game, Luke realized. He remembered one winter when Matthew and Mark had brought home a chess set from school. They'd had a blizzard after that, and they'd been snowed in for a long time, so Matthew and Mark spent hours playing chess. Luke had been a lot younger then, maybe only five or six. The game that fascinated his brothers only puzzled him.

"Why don't all the pieces move the same way?" he had asked, picking up the horse-shaped piece. "Why can't this one go in a straight line like the castle?"

"Because it can't," Matthew had replied irritably, while Mark squealed, "Put that down! You're messing up our game!"

Now Luke almost trod on another boy's heel. The boy didn't even turn around. If everyone at the school were a chess piece, Luke realized, most of the boys were pawns. The hall monitors and the other ones Luke thought of as starers were the big, important pieces. The bishops. And the king. Luke remembered that Matthew and Mark had treasured those pieces, sacrificing pawns and knights and castles to protect them. But Luke hadn't understood why. And he didn't understand the hall monitor now.

But he knew how to find out about him.

CHAPTER *EIGHTEEN*

When dinner was over that night, Luke slipped out of the dining hall behind all of the other boys. Instead of going into the evening lecture room like everyone else, he ducked down a dark hall. It wasn't a direct route to the door that led outside, but if Luke turned three corners and backtracked a bit, he'd get there.

I know the school really well now, Luke marveled. *If I had a note I needed to read in private now, it wouldn't be a problem at all.*

Luke felt decades older than the scared little boy who'd worried so over the note from Jen's dad. And gotten so upset when he read it.

It was just a scrap of paper. What did I expect?

Luke wondered: Would he ever look back on this day and regret getting so upset about his ruined garden?

No.

Luke had told himself it didn't matter if he ran into hall monitors. He could just start asking them questions: *Why did you destroy my garden? What if I told*

M A R G A R E T   P E T E R S O N   H A D D I X

the headmaster that you've been sneaking out? But now, creeping down the deserted hallway, he was glad he didn't have to test his bravado. As far as he could tell, the hall monitors only guarded the main route to the door. He'd suspected as much. The monitors didn't have to be very cautious, because most of the boys at the school behaved like sheep, only going where they were told. And all of the teachers seemed to be gone in the evenings.

Luke reached the final corner before the doorway, and stopped. The sound of his watch ticking seemed to fill the entire hall. Luke pressed his wrist to his chest to muffle it. Then it was his heart pounding that seemed too loud. His ears roared with listening.

Was this how Jen had felt, the night she left for the rally? Brave, reckless, crazy, courageous, terrified—all at once?

It didn't seem right to compare. Jen had been going to the rally—leading it, in fact—in an effort to win rights for third children all over the nation. Even her parents didn't know what she was doing. But she had believed so strongly that nobody should have to hide that she'd died for it.

Luke was mad about a garden.

Thinking that way, Luke felt foolish. He wondered if he should turn around. But just because Jen's cause had been enormous, that didn't mean Luke's was unimportant. Like Jen, Luke wanted to right a wrong.

Just then he heard the sounds he'd been waiting for: someone whispering, a muffled laugh, the click of the door latching. Luke waited a full five minutes—it was too dark to see his watch, so he counted off the tics. Then he tip-toed out of the shadows and followed the others out the door.

CHAPTER *NINETEEN*

T he moon was out.

It had been so long since Luke had seen the night sky that he'd forgotten how mystical it could look. The moon was full tonight, a beautiful orb hovering low over the woods. Luke also recognized the same pinpricks of starlight he'd been used to seeing back home. But the stars seemed dimmer here, overshadowed by a glow on the horizon beyond the woods. Luke puzzled over that glow— it was in the wrong part of the sky to be the sunset. What else was that bright?

Luke remembered that Jen's dad had said the school was near a city. Could a city have lights that bright, that shone this far?

"I don't know anything," Luke whispered to himself. He'd thought that coming out of hiding would expose him to the world, teach him everything. But being at Hendricks seemed like just another way to hide.

A light flashed in the woods just then, and Luke realized he didn't have time to hesitate. He'd planned to creep across the lawn, but the moonlight was so bright, he worried about being seen. He decided to take his chances with running.

Nobody yelled. Nobody hissed, "Get away from here!"

Luke reached the edge of the woods and hid behind a tree. Then he cautiously moved up to the next tree. And the next one. The light swung erratically, just ahead.

Luke wished he'd taken the time to explore the woods, to get his bearings. He was terrified of walking straight into a tree, stepping in some big hole or tripping over a stump. He banged his shin and had to bite his lip to keep from crying out. He stepped in something squishy and almost fell. He wondered if he was traveling in circles.

Then he heard voices.

"—hate nature—"

"Yeah, well, you find a better place to meet—"

Luke crept closer. And closer. A strangely familiar voice was giving a long explanation: "—it's just your fear of the outdoors cropping up again. You've got to overcome it, you know?"

"Easy for you to say," someone else grumbled.

Luke was close enough now to see the backs of several heads. He dared to edge up to the next tree and peek out. Eight boys were sitting in a semicircle around a small, dim, portable lantern. Suddenly another light flashed on the other side of the group of boys. A twig cracked. Luke ducked back behind the tree.

"So what's with the emergency meeting?"

It was a girl's voice.

Luke inhaled sharply.

Jen . . .

It wasn't Jen, of course. When Luke dared to look out again, he saw a tall, scrawny girl with two pale, thin braids hanging on either side of her face. Jen had been shorter, more muscular, her brown hair cut short as a boy's. But just to hear a girl's voice again made Luke feel strange. It kept him from doing any of the crazy things he'd half-planned: leaping from behind the tree and screaming accusations, pretending to be a ghost haunting the woods, finding some way to exact revenge.

All he could do now was listen.

"Sorry to disturb the princesses of Harlow," a male voice was answering mockingly.

Luke knew he knew that voice. He peered out. Yes. Of course.

Jackal boy.

"It's the new kid," jackal boy was saying. "He's acting weird."

I should have known jackal boy was involved, Luke thought. *He probably planned the whole thing, led the charge on my garden. . . .* He glowered. Then he realized what jackal boy had said. "The new kid"? As far as Luke knew, there was only one new kid at Hendricks: himself. They were talking about him.

"Weird?" the girl's voice replied. "He's a boy, right? Isn't weirdness just kind of required?"

There were giggles. Luke squinted into the darkness. He

thought there were three or four other girls beside the girl with braids.

"Quit being such an exnay," jackal boy said.

"Exnay and proud of it," the girl retorted.

Luke listened harder, as though that would help him make sense of their words. Who would be proud of being an "exnay"? If he'd learned anything at Hendricks, it was that "exnay" was one of the worst insults you could hurl at anybody.

"Yeah, yeah. I don't see you announcing it anywhere but in the dark, in the woods, when nobody's around," jackal boy taunted.

"So you're admitting you're nobody?" the girl said.

One of the boys beside jackal boy made a frustrated grunt. "Why do we bother talking to them?" he asked.

Luke saw jackal boy dig his elbow into the other boy's ribs.

"I'll be noble and ignore that," jackal boy said loftily to the girl. "Naturally, we don't expect you to offer us any assistance in this matter. But we thought it was in everybody's best interest to keep you informed."

The girl sat down, and the other girls followed her lead. "So inform us."

"The new boy—" jackal boy started.

"Has he got a name?" the girl interrupted.

"He's registered as Lee Grant," jackal boy said.

Luke noticed how he said that. "Registered as . . ." Not, "His name is . . ." Did jackal boy suspect?

"I looked him up," jackal boy continued. "His dad's in charge of National Gas and Electric. Filthy rich. And he's switched schools a lot."

"That could fit," the girl said.

"But he doesn't seem like he has autism or any of the other disorders. I don't think he's even agoraphobic."

Luke didn't even try to puzzle out the unfamiliar words. Jackal boy was still talking.

"Trey over there saw him coming in from outside this afternoon."

"He was outside?" the girl asked. She sounded amazed, maybe even impressed. "Out here? In the woods? During the day?"

"Don't know," jackal boy said. Luke felt almost triumphant at the note of misery in the boy's voice. But Luke was confused. Had jackal boy and his friends destroyed the garden without even knowing it belonged to Luke? Or was jackal boy lying?

"Trey didn't see him until he was back inside," jackal boy continued. "He—you know—he doesn't like looking right at the door."

"Great guard system you got going there," the girl said.

"Shut up, Nina!" one of the boys yelled. Luke guessed it was Trey.

"Don't call me that!" the girl—Nina?—yelled back. Why would she have a name she didn't want to be called?

And then Luke understood. He, too, had a name he hated. He hated it because it was fake. And so was hers.

"Nina" was another former shadow child. She had to be.

Luke looked with new eyes at the group sitting in front of him in the dark woods. They must all be illegal third children using false identities. Luke's heart gave a jump. At last, he'd found others like him. He'd found a place to belong.

Luke started to move out from behind the tree, to reveal himself. Finally he'd found other kids to talk to about how hard it was pretending to be someone else. Finally he'd found other kids who would know how tough it was to come out of hiding. Finally he'd found other kids he could trust, as he'd trusted Jen. They could grieve for Jen with him.

Then he remembered: He was almost certain these were the ones who'd destroyed his garden.

Luke stayed put.

"All right, all right," jackal boy was saying. "Calm down. The point is, this kid, this 'Lee,' doesn't fit any of the profiles."

"Did you give him the test?" Nina asked.

"Um, well, there was a little problem—" jackal boy said hesitantly.

"Go ahead and say it!" Trey burst out furiously. "I flubbed the whole thing! I don't know why you make me guard that spot!"

"Because you're the bravest one," jackal boy said. Luke recognized that tone: It was the same sort of wheedling voice that Luke's brothers had used on him when they wanted him to do something unpleasant, like clean out the hog pen or spread manure on the garden.

Trey turned and faced Nina directly. "I left the door open, but I couldn't stand to be that close to it. I walked down the hall. Just for a minute! When I got back, this Lee kid was nowhere in sight."

Left the door open . . . Suddenly Luke understood. That first time he'd noticed the door, when it was ajar, it had been a test set up by jackal boy's gang.

But what were they testing him for?

"Maybe he went outside then, too," Nina said.

All the boys seemed to be shaking their heads in disbelief.

"I waited for three hours," Trey said. "I stared at that door the whole time, honest. Nobody'd stay out that long."

Why not? Luke wondered.

"So is he one of us or not?" Nina asked.

The question seemed to hang in the dark woods. Luke wanted to know the answer, too.

"Who knows?" jackal boy said. "The problem is, he's getting bold. Weird, like I said. We're scared he's going to get the rest of us in trouble. Blow our cover. This afternoon, he just stared back at Trey like he didn't care what Trey saw, or what Trey did. He was—"

"Defiant," Trey said.

Even Luke could see the baffled look jackal boy gave Trey.

"Sorry!" Trey said. "All I had to do when I was hiding

was read, remember? I didn't have a TV like the rest of you. I learned too many big words. 'Defiant' means, um—he was defying me, he was—"

"Offering a challenge," Luke said aloud.

And then he stepped out from behind the tree.

CHAPTER *TWENTY*

Luke felt twelve pairs of eyes on him. Nina's mouth was frozen in a little "o" of surprise. Jackal boy's jaw dropped in astonishment.

But nobody was more astonished than Luke. *Why did I do that?* he wondered. He remembered thinking that most of the boys at Hendricks acted like pawns. *I'm a pawn, too, remember? Just plain old Luke Garner, who doesn't know anything about anything, who cowers in the attic while his best friend dies for the cause. Stepping out from behind that tree was something Jen would have done. Not me.*

But he had done it. Now what?

Luke longed to slide back behind the tree again or, given that it wouldn't be much of a hiding place now, to turn tail and run. But his legs were trembling so much that just standing still took all his strength.

Everyone was so quiet that Luke could hear his watch ticking again.

All right. He'd gotten himself into this mess by acting like Jen. What would she do next?

Talk. Jen could always talk.

"You destroyed my garden," Luke accused. "You'll have to make restitution."

Luke could use big words, too. He thought he saw a glimmer of appreciation in Trey's eyes. Everyone else stared blankly.

Would Jen bother explaining, or would she prefer letting them feel dumb?

"Garden?" jackal boy asked. "What garden?"

That wasn't what Luke had expected.

"What garden?" he repeated. "*My* garden. Over there." He pointed into the dark. "Last night, somebody trampled the whole thing, kicked over my beans, broke off my raspberry plants. *You're* the only ones I see out in the woods." Luke tried to let his anger carry him through. But all the faces in front of him looked vacant. Had he made a big mistake? Could they possibly be innocent? He finished weakly, "So you owe me."

Jackal boy shook his head.

"We don't know what you're talking about."

He didn't *seem* to be lying. But how good was Luke at judging liars?

"I'll show you," Luke said impatiently. He suddenly had the notion that if he saw them looking at the destruction, he'd be able to tell by their expressions whether or not they were guilty. He turned hastily and started walking. He was surprised when he heard footsteps behind him. They'd actually listened to him? *Obeyed* him?

They made a strange procession through the woods, Luke leading the way, the other boys following with their lantern, then the girls with a dim flashlight. Luke made a few missteps, and even had to backtrack once, but he circled around, hoping none of the others would notice. Finally they reached Luke's clearing. In the moonlight it looked desolate, just a stump and scraggly plants. It didn't look like it had ever contained a garden.

"There!" Luke said, trying to sound wronged and indignant. His voice came out in a squeak. "See these broken-off raspberry plants? See the squashed beans? But why do I have to show you? You know what you did."

No guilt showed on their faces. They still looked puzzled.

"He *is* crazy," jackal boy hissed.

"Wait a minute," Nina said. "Did you guys walk back to school this way last night?"

Trey shrugged.

"We might have," he said.

One of the other guys spoke up.

"It's not like we can tell any of the trees apart."

"So maybe you stepped on his garden by mistake," Nina said. "And didn't even know it."

"*I* certainly wouldn't know what a garden looks like," one of the other girls said. "Like this? What were you growing?"

"Nothing," Luke muttered. He was suddenly overcome with shame. He'd felt so brave stepping out from behind that tree. Just to make a fool of himself. Looking around, he could see how the other boys could have missed noticing his efforts, and trampled his garden by mistake. This had been a pathetic excuse for a garden. He'd been pathetic for ever thinking it was anything, let alone anything worth taking a risk for. He wished he could go back and hide behind a tree forever.

Jackal boy started laughing first.

"You thought this was a *garden?* You were sneaking out here to make a *garden?*" he asked.

The others began to snicker, too. Luke's shame turned into anger.

"So?" he asked, defiant again.

"So you are a lecker," jackal boy said. He was laughing so hard, he doubled over in mirth. "A *real* lecker."

"You always say that," Luke grumbled. "I don't even know what a lecker is."

"Someone from the country," Trey explained helpfully. "Like a bumpkin. That's what it really means. But now the word's just kind of a general insult, like calling someone a moron or stupid."

Luke thought Trey almost sounded apologetic, but that only made things worse.

"What's wrong with being from the country?" Luke asked.

"If you have to ask . . . ," jackal boy said, laughing again. He had to sit down on the rotting stump to catch his breath. Luke hoped he got mold smears on his pants.

"Want to know something even funnier?" jackal boy continued. "I'm betting you're really an exnay, too. So all those insults—lecker, exnay, fonrol—they're all true. I don't know that I've ever met someone who's all three before. We'll have to come up with a new word, just for you. What'll it be?"

Luke stared at jackal boy and the others laughing behind him. His faced burned. How could he have thought, even for an instant, that these might be kids he could trust? That he might belong with them?

"Leave me alone!" he shouted, and turned and ran.

CHAPTER *TWENTY-ONE*

L uke could hear someone crashing through the woods behind him, but he didn't look back. He'd run into the darkest part of the woods, and it took all his concentration to dodge the tree limbs that seemed to reach down out of nowhere. In fact, if Luke really wanted to terrify himself, he could think of those tree limbs as witches' arms, ghouls' fingers. He wasn't used to running through woods at night. Back home, when he'd gone outside after dark, it had mostly been for catching lightning bugs in the backyard, playing moonlight kick ball with his brothers— innocent fun.

He'd been so young, back then, back home.

He forced himself to run faster, but whoever was behind him seemed to be catching up. Luke zigzagged, because he'd read once that that was how rabbits escaped their predators. Then he slammed into a tree. He screamed in pain, and reeled backwards.

A dark shape pounced. Before he knew it, Luke was pinned to the ground.

Luke remembered another time he'd been tackled: the

MARGARET PETERSON HADDIX

first time he'd crept into Jen's house. He made a noise, and the next thing he knew, she had him facedown in the carpet. And they'd become friends.

This wasn't Jen.

"What do you think you're doing?" a voice hissed in his ear. Jackal boy's. "You go back now, during Indoctrination, and they'll catch you. They'll know. And then they'll come looking for the rest of us."

Indoctrination? Luke guessed that jackal boy meant the evening lecture. The name made sense—the lecture was always about how wonderful the Government was. But Luke hadn't even thought about what he was running toward. He was just running away.

"Who will catch me?" he asked. "The only ones who watch are the hall monitors. And they all report to you, right?"

"You got it," jackal boy said. He sounded pleased. "I worked hard setting up that system. The teachers didn't like hall duty, anyway. And now—"

"You can get away with anything, can't you?" Luke asked. "Unless I tell."

He didn't know what possessed him to make that threat. Maybe it was just habit—after twelve years of being the youngest brother, he knew the power of tattling.

And he knew how easily it could backfire.

"Make you a deal," Luke said quickly. "Let me up, and I won't go back now. Answer some questions for me, and I won't tell. I'll keep your secrets."

Jackal boy seemed to be considering. Finally, he said, "Okay."

Luke scrambled up and pulled away. He rubbed the side of his face. He wasn't sure if it was sore from hitting the tree or from being slammed against the ground. His hand came away wet.

"I'm bleeding," he said accusingly.

"You'll have to hide it," jackal boy said. "Are you good at hiding?"

Luke shrugged away the question. He knew jackal boy was really asking something else. But Luke wasn't ready to answer.

"What's your name, anyway?" Luke asked.

"Which one?" jackal boy asked. "If you look at the school records, I'm Scott Renault. Out here, I'm Jason."

"One of those names is fake," Luke said.

Somewhere in the woods, an owl hooted. Luke waited. Finally, jackal boy answered, softly, "Yes."

"Your friends all have fake names, too," Luke said.

"Yes." No hesitation.

"You're all third children who have come out of hiding with fake I.D. cards," Luke said.

"Exnays," jackal boy said.

"Is *that* what that means?" Luke asked.

"You didn't know?" jackal boy asked. "Where have you been all your life?"

Luke decided not to answer that question, either.

"And fonrols—" he started.

"—are any third children, hiding or not."

"Why does everyone at school call each other those names?" Luke asked. "Is everyone here an exnay?"

In the dark, Luke could barely see jackal boy shaking his head.

"Haven't kids called each other exnays and fonrols at the other schools you've been to? All the other places you've ever lived? Some say in the beginning the Government paid people to use 'fonrol' and 'exnay' as swear words. On TV, and stuff. Then those words were forbidden in public broadcast, which just meant that people used them more in private. They wanted to make sure that everyone thought of third children as terrible."

Luke wondered why Jen had never told him about that.

"Maybe I've never been to any other schools," Luke said cautiously. He'd said "maybe." He could still deny everything if he wanted.

Jackal boy laughed, openmouthed. His teeth glinted in the moonlight.

"Why don't you just come out and admit it?" he asked. "You're an exnay, too. I know it."

Luke dodged the question.

"Why do you harass me every night?" he asked. "When everyone else ignores me—"

"It's the procedure we developed for dealing with new boys," jackal boy said. "And new girls, over at Harlow School for Girls. We've discovered it's hard for shadow children when they first come out of hiding—they're overwhelmed, traumatized. Think about it. They've spent their whole lives thinking it's death to be seen, and suddenly they're expected to interact with others all day long, to sit through classes with dozens of other kids, behave normally. They freak out."

"Did you?" Luke asked, trying to picture jackal boy as the new kid, just come out of hiding, scared of everything. His imagination failed him.

"Me?" Jackal boy sounded surprised. "Sure. It was tough. The problem was, lots of exnays got so panicked, they'd do something really dumb—stand up and chant their real name, start screaming, 'Don't look at me! Don't look at me!'—you know, totally lose it. Now, Hendricks has a lot of disturbed kids, anyway—"

"It does?" Luke asked.

"Haven't you noticed?" Jackal boy sounded amazed. "The autistic kids—the ones who rock and won't look you in the eye—the phobic kids, we've got all sorts of troubled cases in there. Ever meet Rolly Sturgeon? *There's* a psycho for you. So exnays can get away with some pretty wacky behavior at Hendricks. But the Population Police still got in a few good raids. That's why a lot of us exnays got together and planned it all out. Every time a new kid arrives, we go into emergency mode until we can tell if he's an exnay or not. We watch. We protect." Luke remembered the hands pushing him down into the chair that first day, in his first class. "But we do it all in secret. We give the exnay plenty of breathing room. And we pick just one person to approach him. To be a friend."

Luke thought about having to chant, "I am a fonrol" fifty times, of having to do push-ups while everyone else laughed, of having to obey every single one of jackal boy's sarcastic commands.

"I thought friends were supposed to be nice to you," Luke said bitterly. "Maybe that's a word I don't understand, either."

"Being too nice to an exnay from the start only causes trouble," jackal boy said. "They break down. They get weepy. They're so happy to find a sympathetic ear that they tell everything, no matter who else can hear. No, exnays need the kind of friend who can toughen them up. Like I did for you."

Was that what had happened? Luke felt as overwhelmed and confused as he had his first day at Hendricks. Listening to jackal boy was like it used to be listening to Jen: They were both so sure of themselves, it was hard for Luke to figure out what he thought on his own.

"How can you tell if a new kid is an exnay or not?" Luke asked, stalling.

"We give them a test," jackal boy said. "When they're ready, we leave a door open and make sure they see it, we stare them right in the eye—we know exactly how an exnay would respond, compared with a typical agoraphobe, or a typical autistic kid."

"You've got everyone figured out, huh?" Luke said.

"Sure," jackal boy asked. "Can't you tell?"

Luke couldn't answer that question. He was feeling panicky again. In a minute, he was going to have to make a decision. With Jen, it had been easy—he'd trusted her right away. But he was older now, more suspicious. He knew that she had been betrayed.

And he could be, too.

"So you gave me the usual test," he said tentatively. "Did I pass?"

"Depends on what you call passing," jackal boy said. He sounded cagier now, like he wasn't sure whose side Luke was on.

Luke had run out of questions. Or—he had lots of questions, but none of them would help him decide whether to trust jackal boy and his friends with his secret. It would be so nice to be able to tell. But was it worth risking his life for?

Had he already risked his life by following them into the woods?

Luke didn't like thinking things like that. He missed Jen all of a sudden. She was always good at turning his fear into a joke.

"Did you know Jen?" he asked jackal boy abruptly.

"Jen?" jackal boy said, his voice suddenly exuberant. "Jen Talbot? You knew her, too?"

Luke nodded. "She was my, um, neighbor. I went over to her house whenever I could," he said.

"Wow," jackal boy breathed. "Come on!"

He grabbed Luke's arm and pulled him back through the woods, all the time marveling, "I can't believe you really met her. In person. It's incredible. She's legendary, you know—"

The low-hanging tree limbs didn't seem so frightening now. Luke and jackal boy simply ducked. Together. A couple times jackal boy held a branch out of the way so Luke could go first. A couple times Luke returned the favor. Jackal boy kept rushing Luke along. They burst back into the clearing where everyone else was still sitting, not even talking. They appeared to have nothing to do but wait for jackal boy.

"Listen, you all!" jackal boy announced. "This is unbelievable! He knew Jen. He went to her house and everything!"

There was a flurry of questions—"What was she like?" "Did she tell you about the rally?" "How did you know her?" Someone produced a bag of cookies and they all passed it around, like it was a party.

It was a party. It was a party where they were accepting Luke into their group. Just because he knew Jen.

Luke did his best to answer all the questions.

"Jen was—amazing," he said. "She wasn't scared of anything. Not the Population Police, not the Government, not anyone. Not even her parents." Luke thought about how strange it was that Jen's father worked for the Population Police. Mr. Talbot was like a double agent, trying to help third children instead of killing them. But he hadn't been able to prevent his own daughter's death. He'd just barely managed to keep the Population Police from finding out that she had been his daughter.

Luke didn't want to talk about Jen's death, just her life.

"She spent months planning the rally," he said. "It was her statement, 'I deserve to exist. We deserve to exist.' She wanted as many third children there as possible. Out of hiding. She thought the Government would have to listen. She took everyone to the steps of the president's house . . ." Luke remembered the fight they'd had when he'd refused to go. And how she'd forgiven him. He stopped talking, lost in grief.

"The Government killed everyone at the rally," Nina finished for him.

Luke nodded blindly. He couldn't ignore Jen's death. He choked out, "Jen was a true hero. She was the bravest person I'll ever know. And someday—someday everyone will know about her."

The others nodded solemnly. *They know how I feel,* Luke marveled. And then, in spite of his grief, he felt a shot of joy: I *am* one of them. I belong.

After that, somehow, he was able to tell happy stories about Jen. He had the whole crowd laughing when he described how Jen had dusted for his fingerprints the first time he'd gone to her house.

"She wanted to make sure I was . . ." Luke hesitated. He had been about to say "another shadow child, like her." But that wasn't how he wanted to reveal his secret, just letting it slip out like it didn't matter. He finished lamely, "She wanted to make sure I was who I said I was."

"So," jackal boy said, lounging against a tree. "Who are you, anyway? What's your real name, 'Lee'?"

Luke looked at the circle of faces surrounding him. Jackal boy's question had silenced the laughter. Or maybe it was Luke's sudden stammering. Now everyone was watching Luke expectantly. An owl hooted somewhere deeper in the woods, and it was like a signal. Finally. It was time to tell.

"L—" Luke started. But the word stuck in his throat. All those nights he'd whispered his name, all those times he'd longed to speak his name aloud—and now he couldn't.

Some of the dry cookie crumbs slid back on his tongue and he started coughing, choking. One of the other boys had to pound him on the back before Luke got his breath back.

"Lee Grant," Luke said, as soon as he could speak again. His urge to confess was gone. "My name is Lee Grant."

"Sure," jackal boy kidded him. "Whatever you say."

And then Luke felt foolish. Jackal boy had revealed his real name. Why couldn't Luke reveal his?

Because, Luke thought with a chill, *I didn't decide to belong. Jackal boy decided for me.*

CHAPTER *TWENTY-TWO*

Belonging to jackal boy's group made all the difference in the world. It began that night. Luke didn't have to creep back from the woods by himself, praying nobody noticed. He went with the others, as part of the crowd. They strutted down the hall, not even trying to be quiet.

"What if someone hears?" Luke ventured.

"Who cares?" jackal boy replied. "Indoctrination's almost over. If there are any teachers around, they'll just think we left early to man our hall monitor posts."

They were in a brighter end of the hall now. Jackal boy got a good look at Luke's face and whistled.

"You really did get all bloody. Come on. I'll take you to the nurse."

Jackal boy led Luke to an unfamiliar office, one he'd seen only once before, when he was searching for windows.

"My friend walked into the wall, coming out of Indoctrination," Jackal boy told the woman who answered the door. "Stupid, huh? Can you give him a bandage?"

"My, my, you boys. You never look where you're going,"

the woman fussed. She was old and wrinkled, like the pictures Luke had seen of grandmothers. She puttered around
getting antiseptic and gauze and tape. Then she dabbed at
Luke's cheek with a wet cloth. "This is an awfully rough
abrasion. Which wall did you run into, dear?"

Jackal boy saved Luke from having to answer.

"Oh, he didn't get bloody from the wall," jackal boy
explained. "He kind of bounced off the wall and fell down.
Then he scraped his face on the carpet. Someone might
have kicked him by mistake, too."

Luke's mother would have listened to an excuse like that
and then said, "Okay. Now. What really happened?" But
this woman only nodded and *tsk-tsked* a little more.

The antiseptic stung, and Luke had to bite his lip to
keep from crying out. But the woman was quick, and his
face was neatly bandaged before he knew it.

"Write your name and the time down in the log on
your way out," the woman said. "And be more careful the
next time, all right?"

Jackal boy even wrote Luke's name for him.

Up in their room, jackal boy stretched and yawned and
proclaimed, "I don't feel like dealing with the new kid
tonight. Let's just leave him alone. Okay, guys? He's getting
boring, anyway."

Luke thought some of his other roommates looked disappointed, but nobody complained.

In the morning, jackal boy said, "You can have breakfast
with us. We have our own table. Hall monitor privileges."

"But I'm not a hall monitor," Luke said.

"The teachers won't notice," jackal boy said. "And maybe you will be soon."

So Luke sat at a table with other boys. For once he didn't have to force himself to choke down his oatmeal. It practically tasted good. And for the first time, Luke got a good look around the dining hall without feeling like he had to glance quickly and furtively. With clean white walls and a peaked ceiling, it really wasn't such a bad place.

"Can I ask you some questions? Here, I mean," Luke said to jackal boy.

"As long as you're not acting like a real exnay," jackal boy said brusquely, as if he were truly swearing at Luke. But Luke caught the double meaning. It was a brilliant code.

"Why is this school like this?" Luke began. "I mean, with no windows, and the strange boys . . . and the teachers who don't seem to notice us unless we do something wrong. And even then, they just say, 'Two demerits.' I don't even know what that means."

Jackal boy pushed back his oatmeal and smirked.

"Confusing, huh?" he asked mockingly. But he started explaining, anyway. "Hendricks began as an educational experiment. Back when there were the famines, people had debates about whether the undesirables in society deserved food when so many were starving. They let all the criminals die, but a bunch of bleeding-heart, sympathetic types said it was cruel not to feed people with mental illnesses, physical disabilities, that kind of thing.

One man stepped forward and offered his family's estate to be two schools for troubled kids. Hendricks for boys and Harlow for girls. He said he'd feed them, too—you see how well he's doing." Jackal boy made a face at the oatmeal. "They built the schools without windows because Mr. Hendricks had the idea that kids with agoraphobia—the ones scared of wide-open spaces—would be better off not even seeing the outdoors. He thought they'd start longing for what they couldn't see. And he thought having windows would just overstimulate the autistic kids. But he also thought it'd be good to bring in some normal kids. Like role models."

Luke tried to absorb all of that. He thought about how differently jackal boy acted when he was explaining something, compared with how Jen had always been. Jen was always outraged, indignant over every little injustice. He could just hear her voice, rising in disgust: "Can you believe it? Isn't that terrible?"

Jackal boy just sounded secretly amused, almost haughty. Too bad. Poor kids. Who cares?

Luke swallowed another bite of lumpy oatmeal.

"And the teachers?" he prompted. "Why aren't they more . . . um . . ."

"Involved? Aware? Semi-intelligent?" jackal boy offered.

"Yeah. All the adults. Like, the nurse last night didn't seem very smart. And what's-her-name, in the office, when I was in there the first day, it was like all the students were just a pain to her."

"Think about it," jackal boy said. "If you were a grown-up, and you could get a job anywhere else, would you work here? We got the dregs, man, the real dregs."

Luke didn't know anything about grown-up jobs. He'd never thought he would be able to come out of hiding to have one.

Jackal boy was smirking again. "But it serves our purposes, all right, to have teachers who are just one step up from leckers. We can do just about anything we want. Got it?"

He looked around at his cohorts, the hall monitors, and soon they were all smirking, too.

Luke wanted to object to that word, "lecker." Just because someone came from the country, that didn't make him dumb. Did it?

Something else bothered Luke, too.

"But I wanted to learn a lot at Hendricks," he said. "Math and science and how to speak other languages. . . . I've been here a month and I haven't learned a thing. I don't even know if I'm going to the right classes. I wanted to—" he broke off at the last minute because he remembered he couldn't talk about being an exnay. He couldn't say that he wanted to learn everything he could to help make third children legal again.

Jackal boy was laughing anyway.

"Oh, right, we're all here to learn," he said, rolling his eyes. This made his friends laugh, too. "Just stick close to me," jackal boy continued. "That's how you learn what you need to know. Forget the classes. And if you're worried about grades—don't you think I know how to fix that, too? How do you think we all got on the honor roll?"

Luke didn't know. He didn't even know what the honor roll was.

But when the bell rang for the first class, he left the dining hall with jackal boy and his gang. He felt safe now, traveling in a pack. All the hall monitors he passed gave him knowing looks, with secret nods that nobody else could have noticed.

And when he hesitated between classrooms, jackal boy was quick to tell him where to go.

CHAPTER TWENTY-THREE

uke didn't go back to his garden by himself anymore. But two or three times a week, jackal boy would whisper in his ear, "Tonight," and Luke's heart would jump. "Tonight" meant, "We're going to the woods. We're meeting the girls."

Each time he stepped outside, Luke would breathe in deeply, the same way a starving man gobbled down food. But he noticed that most of the others, all so brave and imposing indoors, positively cowered in the open air. They squeezed their eyes shut and took halting steps forward, like condemned men walking to their executions.

"You don't like the outdoors, do you?" Luke asked Trey once as they walked across the lawn to the woods.

Trey shook his head slowly, as if moving too quickly might make him throw up. He looked a little green already.

"It's better in the woods," he said through gritted teeth. "At least there we're covered."

"But—" Luke took another deep breath, savoring the smell of newly mowed grass and spring rain. He couldn't understand Trey. "Don't you hate being cooped up all the time?"

Trey gave him a sidelong glance.

"I spent thirteen years in the same room. I didn't step foot outside even once until I came here."

"Oh," Luke said. He suddenly saw that, for a third child, he'd been very lucky. Before the Government tore down the woods behind his house and built a neighborhood there instead, he'd spent most of his time outdoors. Except for not going to school, he hadn't lived that differently from his older brothers.

He couldn't imagine spending thirteen years in the same room.

"Jen went shopping on fake passes," he told Trey. "Her mother took her to play groups. I thought other third children lived like her."

"I wouldn't know," Trey said. "I—I wished—" He hesitated. "I miss my room."

Luke felt sorry for the other boy. How many of his other new friends had basically lived their entire lives in a box?

He watched jackal boy running ahead, then circling back to encourage the others.

"Jacka—I mean, Jason must have been like Jen," Luke said. "He must have gotten out a lot. He's not afraid of anything."

"No," Trey said. "He's not. He says he's overcome all his hiding-related phobias. And he's only been here a few weeks longer than you."

"He has?" Luke asked in surprise. He'd assumed jackal

boy was a long-timer, with years of experience at Hendricks.

"The rest of us only started last fall," Trey continued. "I think. No one talked much before Jason got here."

Before he could make sense of that, Luke had to remind himself all over again that "Jason" was really jackal boy. It was no wonder that Luke had been confused when he first started at Hendricks—the boys, at least the ones he hung out with now, did go by three or four different names. They might answer to the first or last part of their fake name at school, and the first or last part of their real name out in the woods. That was riskier. A few just went by initials.

Trey had explained that his name just meant "three." He wouldn't tell even jackal boy his real name.

They reached the woods, and what Trey had said finally sunk in.

"Wait a minute," Luke said. "You mean you weren't all friends before Jason came? You haven't been meeting in the woods all along?"

Trey flashed him a puzzled look.

"Just since April," he said.

Luke's mind was racing.

"The rally was in April," he said.

"Yeah," Trey said with a shrug.

The girls met them then, and they started the same kind of banter Luke had witnessed the first night. It sounded different to Luke now, not as if they were all worldly and experienced, but as if they were reading lines in a play, pretending to talk to each other the way normal boys and girls talked. Nina made jokes about how stupid boys were, and Jason made fun of the girls. Luke watched the faces of the ones who were quiet. They all looked scared.

"What's this meeting for?" Luke asked suddenly.

Jason turned to look at Luke in surprise.

"Why—we're planning ways to resist the Government over the Population Law. To follow up the rally."

"The rally," Nina echoed wistfully.

Luke's heart beat fast. This was what he'd wanted! He'd wanted to do something brave like Jen. It would be like apologizing to her for not going with her, for doubting her.

But could he be as brave as Jen?

Without dying, too?

"How?" he demanded. "How are we going to resist?"

Nina and Jason looked at each other.

"Well, that's what we're deciding," Nina said. "Just like a boy, asking dumb questions!"

But they didn't decide anything that night. They just joked around some more, made a game of guessing one boy's real name, and headed back to their schools.

Jason pulled Luke aside as they stepped back into the school building.

"Not everyone's as ready as you," he said. "You've got to give the others time. As long as they're trembling in their shoes every time they step outside, they'll never make good subversives."

Luke was flattered. It made sense.

"Okay," he said.

Jason playfully punched Luke's arm.

"Knew you'd understand. Hey—you ready for finals?"

"Finals?" Luke asked.

"You know, next week? End-of-term tests?" Jason said. "You pass, you get out of here, you fail, you're stuck for life?"

Luke stopped short.

"Oh, no . . . ," he breathed.

Jason laughed.

"Scared you, huh? Remember, you stay on my good side, I'll make sure your 'parents' get to look at a brilliant report!"

"I'm not even going to the right classes!" Luke said, panic coursing through his veins. "And I can't ask anyone now. It's been too long—"

"I'll find out for you!" Jason said, laughing again. He was already halfway down the hall.

CHAPTER *TWENTY-FOUR*

Jason was as good as his word. The next morning at breakfast, he handed Luke a computer printout that said, at the top, CLASS SCHEDULE FOR LEE GRANT. It had times, room numbers, teachers' names.

"Where'd you get this?" Luke asked.

"You think your only computer hacker friend is dead?" Jason said.

He meant Jen. Luke had a flash of missing her all over again. He could picture her sitting at the computer, typing fast. She'd created a chat room for third children, with the password of "free." She'd connected hundreds of third children, so they weren't just sitting in their little rooms, all alone. She'd hacked into the records of the national police, to make sure none of the kids going to the third-child rally were caught before they got to the capital.

But what good had all her hacking done?

"Earth to Lee," Jason was saying. "Or whatever your name is. You should know, your schedule really doesn't matter. I can change all your grades on the computer, anyhow."

But after breakfast, Luke determinedly marched off to his first class, listened closely, and took detailed notes. By the end of the hour, he knew something he'd never known before: Prime numbers could be divided only by themselves and one.

In his second class, he boldly grabbed a textbook off the bookshelf and read the poem whose page number the teacher had written on the board. He could even make sense of the fancy language—two people were friends, and one of them died, and the other one felt sad.

Luke figured he had an unfair advantage, understanding that.

In science and technology class, the teacher was talking about gasoline motors. Luke could just picture one, all grease-covered, in Father's tractor. And now he knew how they worked.

By lunchtime, Luke was ready to brag to Jason, "I *am* learning something now." He was even confident enough to tease, "Maybe I won't need your help with my grades."

"You're going to learn a whole term's worth in just a week?" jackal boy mocked. "Right. Next week, Friday, at five o'clock, you'll come begging, 'Please, please, I need help! I'll do anything!'"

Luke only set his jaw and pulled out a book to study.

CHAPTER *TWENTY-FIVE*

B y the end of the week, all the teachers had test dates written in chalk on their blackboards. And Luke was spending every spare moment studying.

"Why?" Trey asked him one night as they were trudging out to the woods. "Jason can fix your grades. And it's not like your real parents are going to see them, anyway."

"When you were stuck in your room," Luke said, "didn't you ever want to know anything about the outside world? About whether other people were like you, or different, or whether grass grows the same way all over the world, or how a car runs?"

"Not really," Trey said.

Luke was sorry that he couldn't explain. It wasn't the grades themselves that mattered to him. But he felt like he had something to prove. Maybe that people from the country—leckers—weren't so dumb, after all. Maybe that Jen's dad hadn't risked his life for nothing, getting Luke a fake identity. Maybe that Luke wasn't wasting time just hanging out in the woods making jokes with the girls from Harlow while other third children still had to hide.

He was surprised that, with each day that passed, his classes made more sense to him. The teachers weren't really that bad, just distant. The history teacher, Mr. Dirk, could tell fascinating stories about kings and knights and battles, and they were all true. The literature teacher could recite whole poems from memory. Luke didn't always understand all the words, but he liked the cadence and rhyme. The math teacher said once, "Aren't numbers *friendly?*" and he really seemed to believe it. Luke wondered if the teachers were shy, too—if they had some of those phobias Trey and Jason had talked about, and were downright terrified of looking their students straight in the eye.

The night before his first test, Luke studied through dinner, and skipped going to the woods with all the others during Indoctrination so he could hunch over in a hall-way, reading history. Jason mocked him—"What are you trying to do, bookworm? Learn as many big words as Trey?" and, "You could read all night and still not pass your tests. Come on."

"Leave me alone," Luke growled, eager to get back to the Trojan War.

Luke was surprised that Jason stepped back instead of insisting.

"Fine," he said. "Waste your time. See if I care."

The words sounded like the swaggering boy Luke was used to. But his tone seemed to say something else. So did the set of his shoulders as he walked away. He sounded wary, on edge.

Could Jason possibly be scared of Luke?

Luke was nobody. Jason was in charge. Luke decided he was imagining things, and went back to his book.

Still, after lights out, Luke couldn't sleep. He was too unsettled—worried about the test the next day, wondering what his family was doing back home, wishing Jen were there to figure out Jason for him. He even thought back to the advice Jen's dad had written for Luke: "Blend in." Who was Luke supposed to blend in with? The boys who trudged blindly through the halls each day? The ones who followed Jason? Or Jason himself?

Somewhere in the room, a bed creaked.

Luke thought it was just someone turning over in his sleep but he stiffened anyway, and listened hard.

There was a *pat-pat-pat* that could have been footsteps, or could have been Luke's imagination. And then, the hall light shone briefly into the room as the door was opened and closed.

Luke sat up. He crept over to the door and opened it a crack so he'd have light to see by.

All the beds were filled with sleeping boys except two. Luke's.

And Jason's.

CHAPTER TWENTY-SIX

Luke took time to grab one of his textbooks so he'd have an excuse if someone caught him out of his room after lights out. "I only wanted to study some more," he could say. "I'm worried about my tests."

But the only person who might catch him was Jason.

Out in the dimly lit hall Luke looked back and forth, not sure which way to go. Probably Jason had only needed to go to the bathroom, and Luke was foolish to follow him. Luke headed toward the bathroom first.

Why didn't I think to go to the bathroom after lights out, back when I was trying to find a place to read my note? Luke wondered. But Luke had been too terrified back then to think like that. He wouldn't have dared leave his bed. He had actually blended in quite well. *And if I'd read the note right away, I wouldn't have discovered the door to outdoors or the woods. I wouldn't have had those few days of setting up my garden.* He still missed his garden. He tried not to think about it. *And I never would have gotten to know anybody.*

But how well *did* he know his new friends? The only

MARGARET PETERSON HADDIX

friend he'd ever had before was Jen, and that friendship had been entirely different.

It wasn't fair to compare.

He sneaked quietly down the hall, feeling foolish. Of course Jason would be in the bathroom, and he'd only have rude comments and mockery for Luke when he saw him. "Can't even pee without your books, huh?" maybe, or even, "Hey, lecker, we've got toilet paper here and everything. You won't need to use that."

The bathroom was empty.

Luke backtracked, and glanced in his room again. Jason's bed was still empty. Luke went the opposite direction from the bathroom. All that lay down this hallway was the back stairs.

Maybe Luke wouldn't look for Jason anymore. What did he think he was going to do when he found him? But Luke was so thoroughly awake now that he decided he might as well study. The details of the Trojan War and the Peloponnesian War were blurring in his mind.

He went over to the stairwell and sat down on the top step. He leaned against the wall, opened his book, and began reading. "The Greeks fought battles for—"

Far below Luke, someone was murmuring.

Luke sat still for a minute, tempted to ignore it. It probably was Jason, but so what? If he was having a secret meeting without Luke, why should Luke care? It wasn't like Jason's gang ever planned anything real, anyway.

But Luke did care. If Jason's gang was going to help

third children, Luke owed it to himself—to his family, to Jen, to Jen's dad—to take part.

Luke eased down to the next step. And the next. And the next. He kept clutching his book because he didn't want to make any noise putting it down. Yet he wondered if he should be making noise, acting normal, so he could come upon the secret meeting casually, "Oh, hi, guys—didn't know you were down here. Can I help?"

There was nothing normal about walking around Hendricks in the middle of the night. Luke stayed quiet.

When he rounded the corner of the second flight of stairs, he could begin to distinguish words. The only person who seemed to be talking was Jason. Nothing new about that. Luke crouched behind the half-wall that surrounded the stairs. He listened closely.

"But it's too soon!" Jason was pleading.

Luke risked a peek over the banister. Maybe Trey was there, and would call out, "Hey, Lee! Glad you're here! I was hoping you would come!"

But Jason appeared to be alone.

He was talking into a small portable phone. At least, that's what Luke thought it was. He'd never seen one before, except in sketches in his science textbook.

Jason was facing the other way, so Luke kept watching and listening.

"I told you. There's no danger in waiting!" he exclaimed. "They're just sitting ducks!"

Jason was silent, listening. He turned slightly and Luke

caught a glimpse of the side of his face. Jason's expression was set, dead serious. Luke thought about all the times he'd seen Jason joking, joshing, prodding, mocking. Luke wouldn't have thought Jason could be 100 percent serious about anything. He seemed like a different boy.

Frightened, Luke ducked out of sight.

"I've got four and she's got two," Jason said. "But I could have more by the end of the week."

Four and two and more of what? Luke wondered.

"Well, I don't know about Nina," Jason said. "You'd have to ask her. But she says girls are harder to recruit."

Girls? Luke thought he'd solved his puzzle. Jason was making plans for some action against the Government—something like the rally, but safer, Luke hoped. He was telling someone how many boys and girls—how many exnays—were available to help. Except . . . the group that met in the woods had nine boys now, with Luke, and five girls.

Hadn't Jason told Luke once that the whole group wasn't brave enough yet to be subversives? Luke wondered whom Jason was counting and whom he was leaving out. Trey was pretty timid. So were several of the others.

What about Luke? What if Jason wasn't including Luke because Luke hadn't gone to the meeting in the woods that evening? Or because he knew that Luke was secretly the biggest chicken of all?

Luke started to stand up, to say, "Wait! Count me in!" His legs were quivering, but he could make himself be brave. He'd have to.

Jason had his back turned to Luke again. He was practically snarling into the phone now.

"You want names? All right, I'll give you the ones I have. Antonio Blanco, alias Samuel Irving. Denton Weathers, alias Travis Spencer. Sherman Kymanski, alias Ryan Mann. Patrick Kerrigan, alias Tyrone Janson."

Jason was saying the boys' real names. Luke was so thrilled, he couldn't speak. If only he'd told Jason his real name. He could just imagine hearing, "Luke Garner, subversive for the cause, coming to the aid of third children everywhere." Forget the alias. It didn't matter.

Jason shifted his portable phone in his hand, and Luke had a terrible thought. What if Jason's phone was bugged? Then Luke realized something even worse: Since it was a portable phone, the Population Police didn't even have to bug it. Luke had learned in science and technology class just last week that portable phones sent out messages indiscriminately. Didn't Jason know that? All the Population Police needed was a receiver.

And of course they had one. They had everything.

Luke rushed out from his hiding place and took the last flight of stairs in two leaps. He had to get the phone away from Jason before he accidentally betrayed another boy's identity. Jason still had his back to Luke. He was saying indignantly into the phone: "Of course I'll get the others to tell me their real names. They're just cagey. They do trust me. They don't have any idea I work for the Population Police."

CHAPTER *TWENTY-SEVEN*

uke had his hand inches from the phone when Jason's words registered: " . . . I work for the Population Police." Luke's hand and arm kept going, even though his mind was suddenly frozen. He watched his hand as if it belonged to someone else. His fingers grasped the phone, jerked it out of Jason's grip, and threw it to the ground. Then someone's foot—no, Luke's foot, acting as independently as his hand—stomped on it.

Jason whirled around.

"You!" he spat.

Luke's frozen mind was struggling to thaw. Strange facts were emerging from the ice. Jason worked for the Population Police. That's why he hadn't cared about using a portable phone. He wasn't organizing subversive activity against the Government. He was turning in the exnays.

"You're an informer," Luke whispered.

Jason's eyes narrowed, calculatingly. Luke instantly saw his mistake. Why hadn't he played dumb? He could have pretended he hadn't heard Jason's last sentence. He could have acted hurt that Jason was leaving him out. He could have begged for a dangerous assignment.

It wouldn't have been too hard to act dumb. Until two seconds ago, he had been.

"Now, Lee," Jason said cautiously. He seemed to be trying to decide how to play things. Was Luke going to get, "Oh, don't be silly. What would make you think that? Why would I turn anybody in when I'm an exnay, too?" Or, "So you know the truth. That's it. You're dead"?

Jason took a step toward Luke. Luke clutched his history textbook like a shield. Jason came even closer.

And then, without thinking, Luke whipped the book out and swung it at Jason's head with all his might.

Jason crumpled. Knocked sideways, he tried desperately to regain his balance. Luke swung again.

This time, Jason fell backwards. His head hit the stairs with a loud *thunk*. His body rolled down to the landing.

He didn't move.

CHAPTER *TWENTY-EIGHT*

Luke hardly dared to breathe. He held his book high over his head.

Jason still didn't move.

What if Luke had killed him?

Luke knelt down and put his hand in front of Jason's nose. Very, very faintly, he felt bursts of air every few seconds. Jason wasn't dead, only knocked unconscious.

For how long?

Luke wasted time staring at Jason's motionless body. Luke wouldn't have wanted to be a murderer, but everything would be easier if Jason were dead.

Luke could kill him now.

Everything in Luke recoiled against that notion. Jason was the worst kind of fake—an informer, a traitor, someone who pretends to be a friend and then betrays. He probably had as good as killed four boys whose only crime was existing. Jason deserved to die.

But Luke couldn't kill him.

Luke was desperately trying to get his paralyzed brain to come up with another option, when the portable phone rang. The noise echoed in the stairwell as shrilly as a hundred roosters, all crowing at once. It sounded loud enough to wake the dead, not to mention the merely unconscious. Luke grabbed the phone, just to shut it up. It kept ringing. Luke stared at it stupidly. He'd never actually touched a phone before tonight. Didn't they stop ringing when you picked them up? He punched buttons on the phone at random. Finally, miraculously, the noise stopped.

Luke let out a sigh of relief. Why had the phone rung in the first place? Jason had been using it. Then when Luke pulled it away and stomped on it, that must have worked like hanging it up. But for it to start ringing again—

Someone was calling Jason.

Fearfully, Luke put the phone to his ear.

"Hello?" he whispered.

He had a sudden moment of hope. Maybe he'd misunderstood. Maybe Jason hadn't said that he worked for the Population Police, but that the exnays didn't trust him because they thought he *might* work for the Population Police. Or that the exnays didn't trust anyone, because of the Population Police. Maybe the person on the other end of the line was a good guy, working for the cause, worried that something had happened to poor, noble, misunderstood Jason.

"Hello?" Luke whispered again.

"Don't you ever pull that kind of a stunt on me again!" The angry voice on the other end came through the phone as forcefully as a tornado. "You hang up on the Population Police, you're a dead man. We'll kill you even before we kill those four exnays you just turned in."

Luke's hope dissolved. He struggled to keep his mind from dissolving, too. Think, think . . . He'd heard Jen's dad fool the Population Police once. Mr. Talbot had lied so smoothly that even Luke, who knew the truth, was practically convinced.

Luke put his hand over his mouth. He had to make the man on the other end of the line think he was Jason.

"I'm sorry," Luke muttered. "It was a mistake. I accidentally dropped the phone and it shut off by itself." With a little help from Luke's foot.

"What? I can't hear you!" the man yelled.

"It's a bad connection," Luke said, speaking louder. He'd heard Mother and Dad say that all the time. He hoped portable phones could have bad connections, too. "I said I was sorry. I dropped the phone by mistake. I didn't hang up on you. Why would I hang up on you when I'm trying to convince you to give me more time?"

"Whatever," the man growled. Luke could tell: The man didn't care what had happened. He just wanted Jason to grovel. And Luke had done it for him. Luke was good at groveling.

"Here's how it is," the man continued. "We'll give you another day. Then that's it. And, Jason? You get those other boys or else. We've got a quota to fill, you know."

The phone clicked. Luke realized the man on the other end had hung up.

Luke had fooled him. And he'd bought some time. He had another day.

Or until Jason woke up.

CHAPTER TWENTY-NINE

uke slid his hands under Jason's armpits and began dragging him down the stairs. Down was easier than up. And if Jason woke up and started screaming, he'd be less likely to wake somebody if he and Luke were on the first floor.

Of course, if Jason woke up and attacked Luke, there was also less chance Luke could get help on the first floor.

Luke made himself concentrate on pulling the bigger boy. Jason's feet slipped down the first step and hit hard. Jason moaned but didn't open his eyes.

Maybe he's just faking, Luke thought. *Maybe he's wide awake and he's just waiting for the right moment to attack.*

That thought made Luke sweat. But he pulled harder, and got Jason all the way to the bottom of the steps without waking him up.

Next, Luke dragged Jason down the hall. A right turn, a left turn, a right turn. Jason was heavy, and Luke's arms ached. His head ached, too, from trying to plan. He found the door he'd been looking for and forced himself to knock.

"Yes?" a sleepy voice responded.

Luke grimaced. He'd been half-hoping this idea would fail. *Be brave,* he told himself.

"Nurse!" he called out. "It's my—my friend. He's sick."

How could he have called Jason a friend?

Oh, well. He had a lot more lies ahead of him.

The door eased open. The nurse stood there in a ruffled dressing gown.

"Oh, my," she said dimly when she'd taken in the sight of Jason slumped on the floor. Luke tried to hold him up the way a concerned friend would, but it was hard. Luke would have enjoyed dropping him.

"He passed out," Luke said needlessly. "He was having a—a seizure, ranting and raving. He was . . . telling lies. Making up stories." That should help if Jason came to. "I think it's called delirium, what he had. I think staying unconscious is the best thing for him. Can you give him something that will keep him asleep?"

"Oh, my," the nurse repeated, frowning. "Usually, in these circumstances, we want to revive the patient."

It wasn't fair. Now the nurse seemed to know what she was talking about.

"Help me get him inside," she ordered Luke.

The nurse took Jason's legs, and Luke lifted. The strain on his muscles was terrible. Luke was panting by the time they got Jason to a bed in the nurse's office. She immediately began looking him over.

"Did he hit his head?" she asked Luke as she felt Jason's scalp.

Panic bubbled up in Luke's stomach.

"May-Maybe," he said. "He was, um, thrashing around a lot. In his sleep."

"I thought he was ranting and raving," the nurse said, fixing Luke with an unexpectedly sharp stare. "Was he doing that in his sleep, too?"

Luke gulped.

"No. He was thrashing about, and then he woke up, and acted delirious. And then he had a seizure and went unconscious. I think. It happened really fast. It was really scary."

Luke got another idea.

"You know, you should really strap him down in bed, so if he wakes up and starts acting weird again, he won't hurt himself."

"Thanks for the medical advice," the nurse said. She lifted one of Jason's eyelids and shone a flashlight into his eye. Luke held his breath. If Jason woke up now, he could tell the nurse anything he wanted, and she'd believe him. Jason was a much better liar than Luke. Jason's lips moved. Had he mumbled something that the nurse could hear but Luke couldn't? Luke tried to quell his panic. He watched with relief as Jason's eye rolled blindly back in his head. The nurse gently placed the eyelid back against the eye. Jason didn't move.

The nurse sat down at a desk and took up a pen.

"Now. What's your friend's name?" she asked.

"Ja—I mean, Scott Renault," Luke said.

The nurse peered at him doubtfully.

"And your name is—"

"Lee Grant," Luke mumbled.

The nurse was watching him carefully. Too carefully.

"Okay," she said. "Let me type your account of your friend's injury into the computer." She disappeared around a corner. Luke could hear the nurse muttering to herself. Then there was the *clickety-clack* of a keyboard. The sound made him miss Jen. He remembered Jason acting so excited when Luke had mentioned her name. But that had just been an act—an act contrived to get Luke to trust him, to reveal his real name, so Jason could betray him.

Luke's head spun. It was too hard to recast his memories with Jason as a traitor.

The nurse came back.

"Sign this," she said.

Disheartened, Luke signed without reading.

"Now. Why don't you go on back to bed?" the nurse said to Luke. "I'll take good care of your friend. I promise."

That's what Luke was afraid of.

But there was nothing else for him to do but back out of the door.

"Let me know how he is," Luke begged as he left. "And if he says anything crazy—"

"Don't worry," the nurse said. "I've heard plenty of crazy talk around here."

Out in the hallway, Luke wished he'd thought of another plan. Ropes! He could have tied Jason up, and gagged him, and . . . and put him where, exactly? Even the boys who stared at the ground all day would notice a bound and gagged boy lying around. And where was Luke supposed to get ropes and a gag? No, Luke had had to take his chances with the nurse. He just had to hurry even faster now. Who could tell what lies Jason might tell the nurse when he awoke? All Luke knew was, Jason wouldn't cast Luke as the heroic friend who'd carried Jason to help.

Actually, Jason wouldn't even have to lie. All he had to say was that Luke had hit him with a book and knocked him down. That was true, though not the whole truth. And if anyone wanted to investigate, they could examine Luke's book, and—

Luke's book. Stunned by his own stupidity, Luke realized: He'd left his book and Jason's portable phone back on the stairs.

Forgetting to go quietly, Luke raced down the hall, around corners, and back up the stairs. He saw the history textbook cast off in the corner of the landing, where he'd dropped it. He snatched it up and hugged it to his chest like a long-lost friend. Now, to find the phone—

The phone was nowhere in sight.

CHAPTER THIRTY

T he landing was barely a four-by-four square, flat and empty. But Luke walked around it again and again, as if he'd just missed noticing the phone and it was right there, in plain sight.

It wasn't.

Luke looked on each stair below, and even the stairs above the landing—as if the phone could fly. It took forever for his stubborn brain to accept that the phone was missing. Then he sank down on one of the stair steps, puzzling out who might have taken it.

Did Jason have an accomplice?

Luke thought about all the hall monitors, all the boys who'd met in the woods. Now that Jason's true nature had been revealed, Luke couldn't be sure of anyone. Maybe they all worked for the Population Police.

Except for the four boys Jason had betrayed.

Luke was desperately confused, but he could figure out one thing: The missing phone meant those four were in more immediate danger.

And so was Luke.

Luke's first instinct was to hide, to get the other four to hide with him. The woods wouldn't be safe because Jason would lead the Population Police straight there. Was there a safe place in the kitchen? Somewhere in an unused class-room? Some dormitory room off by itself, and unlikely to be searched?

Hiding was no good. In the end, they'd only be found.

Luke had to do something to prevent the Population Police from ever searching. But he didn't even understand what was going on. He had to find someone who knew more than Luke, who could lie better than Luke, who knew how to handle the Population Police.

Jen's dad.

But how was Luke supposed to reach him?

CHAPTER *THIRTY-ONE*

L uke crept back down to the first floor with only the vaguest plan in mind. He needed Mr. Talbot's phone number. He needed a phone. The school office should have both.

The school office was locked.

Luke stood before the ornate door for what felt like hours. The door had a glass panel at the top, so he could see in easily. He could make out the shape of a phone on Ms. Hawkins's desk. He could see old-fashioned file cabinets behind it. Surely there was a file in there with Luke's name on it—his fake name, anyway. Would Mr. Talbot's phone number be listed in there, because he was the one who'd brought Luke to the school? Luke thought so. But it did no good unless Luke could get into the files. And no matter how much he jiggled the knob of the office door, the door held firm.

Desperately, Luke kicked it. But the door was thick, solid maple wood. Nothing flimsy at Hendricks. Even the glass was probably—

Glass. Luke couldn't believe how stupid he was being.

He slammed the glass panel with his textbook, and a satisfying spiderweb of cracks crept across it. He hit it again, a little lower, smashing that portion of the panel.

"And Jason thinks books are useless," Luke muttered to himself. "Take that!"

Luke covered his hand with part of his pajama sleeve and pushed through the bottom of the glass. Only a few shards fell to the ground. The rest of the panel stayed in place. It was high-quality glass. Anything cheap would have shattered completely, and fallen to the ground with an enormous clatter.

Luke reached on through, until he could touch the knob from inside. He turned it—slowly, slowly—until he heard the click he'd been waiting for. He eased the door open and raced to the filing cabinet.

With only the dim light from the hall, Luke couldn't read any of the labels on any of the files. He had to carry them out to the door to see whose they were.

The first batch he pulled had Jeremy Andrews through Luther Benton. He replaced them and moved further back in the file. Tanner Fitzgerald through—yes, there it was. Lee Grant.

Luke was surprised by the thickness of his file, considering how short a time he'd been at Hendricks. The first set of papers were school transcripts from other schools— evidently the ones the real Lee Grant had attended, before he died and left his identity to Luke. There were pictures, too, seven of them, labeled, KINDERGARTEN, GRADE ONE, GRADE

TWO . . . all the way up to grade six. Strangely, the photos really did look like Luke. Same sandy hair, pale eyes, worried look. Luke blinked, thinking he'd been fooled. But when he opened his eyes, the resemblance was still there. Had the real Lee Grant looked that much like Luke?

Then Luke remembered something Jen had told him once, about changing photos on the computer.

"You can make people look older, younger, prettier, uglier—whatever you want. If I wanted to make my own fake I.D., I probably could," she'd bragged.

But Jen had wanted to come out of hiding with her identity intact. She hated the thought of fake I.D.'s.

Staring at the faked pictures, Luke could understand. It was all too strange. He knew he should be reassured by how thoroughly his records had been doctored. But it frightened him instead. There was no sign of the real Luke Garner. Probably even his family would forget him eventually.

Luke didn't have time for self-pity. He turned the page, hoping his admission papers would be next.

They weren't. Instead, there was some sort of a daily log. Luke read in horrified fascination:

April 28—Student withdrawn, surly during entrance interview. Refuses to look interviewer directly in eye. Refuses to answer questions. Sullen behavior. Hostility believed connected to dissociation with parents. Can assume high risk of repeated attempts at running away. Treatment to commence immediately.

April 29—Sullenness continues. Attempts at interaction rebuffed. Teachers report disinterest, hostility.

The log continued in that vein, with an entry for every day Luke had been at Hendricks. There was repeated mention of therapy and treatment, and its success or failure. But Luke had had no entrance interview. He'd had no therapy, no treatment, no attention from the school officials at all. Obviously, this was another faked record.

But who had faked it? And why?

Thoroughly baffled, Luke turned the page. And there was the thick sheaf of his entrance papers.

Mr. Talbot was listed in the second column of the sixteenth page, as an emergency contact.

Luke grabbed the phone and started dialing.

CHAPTER *THIRTY-TWO*

A woman's sleepy voice answered.

"Is Mr. Talbot there?" Luke asked. "I need Mr. Talbot."

"It's three in the morning!" the woman hissed.

"Please," Luke begged. "It's an emergency. I'm a friend of—" He barely managed to stop himself from saying, "Jen's." Mr. Talbot's phone was probably bugged by the Population Police. Maybe the school's phone was now, too. Luke didn't know. But he tried again. "Mr. Talbot is a friend of my parents'."

There was only dead air in response. Then a man's voice, just as sleepy as the woman's.

"Hello?"

It was Mr. Talbot.

Luke wanted to spill out everything, from his first confusing day at Hendricks, to Jason's treachery, to the oddness of the file Luke still held on his lap. If only he could explain all his problems, surely Mr. Talbot could solve them all. But Luke had to choose his words carefully.

"You told me to blend in," he accused, hoping Mr. Talbot

would remember. "I can't. You have to come get me." *And four other boys,* he added silently, as if Mr. Talbot were actually capable of telepathy. If only Luke could just say, flat out, "You need to get four more fake I.D.'s for these friends of mine. And you'll need to protect their families, too." But Luke couldn't think of any code that would clue in Mr. Talbot, without clueing in the Population Police as well.

"Now, now," Mr. Talbot said calmly, sounding like an elderly uncle dispensing wisdom. "Surely school isn't that bad. You need to give it more of a chance. Is this finals week or something?"

Luke couldn't tell whether Mr. Talbot really didn't understand, or whether he was acting for the sake of the bug.

"That's not the problem!" Luke almost screamed. "It's— it's like a problem I had before."

"Yes, problems do seem to repeat themselves," Mr. Talbot said, still sounding untroubled. "Usually, there's some root cause. You need to attack that first."

Was Mr. Talbot speaking in code? Luke hoped so.

"It's all very well to say that," he protested. "But the problems are multiplying. There are four others, now, I have to think about. And they can't wait until the, um, root cause is fixed. This is an emergency. You have to help."

Luke was proud of himself. He couldn't be any clearer than that, not using a potentially bugged phone. Surely Mr. Talbot would understand.

"You children can be so melodramatic," Mr. Talbot said irritably. Now he sounded like a man ripped from sleep at three in the morning for no good reason. "I have every confidence that you can deal with your problems by yourself. Now. Good night."

"Please!" Luke pleaded.

But Mr. Talbot had hung up.

CHAPTER *THIRTY-THREE*

Luke stared at the phone. He'd tried so hard. It wasn't fair that he didn't even know if he'd succeeded or not.

No. He knew. He'd failed.

He'd heard the careless tone in Mr. Talbot's voice. Luke couldn't fool himself into thinking it was all an act, with each word carrying double meaning. It was three in the morning. He'd awakened Mr. Talbot out of a dead sleep. How could he possibly have understood what Luke needed?

Luke dropped the phone and put his face down on Ms. Hawkins's desk. The file he'd been holding on his lap spilled onto the floor, dumping out papers filled with lies. He didn't care. He didn't care that anyone walking by would catch him where he wasn't supposed to be. He was past caring about anything.

Had Jen ever reached this point, planning the rally?

Luke remembered the last time he'd seen her, the night she'd left for the capital. She'd seemed almost unearthly, as if she'd already passed out of the realm she shared with

Luke. And she had. He was still in hiding, and she was about to risk her life to be free.

It was simpler for you, Luke accused silently. *You weren't confused.*

It was hard having a dead hero for a best friend.

I just can't live up to you, Jen, he thought. *I'm not you.*

He wasn't Lee Grant, either. Slowly, just to get rid of them, he began picking up the faked papers and stuffing them back into the file. Moving like someone in a dream, he put the phone back on the desk and the file back in the filing cabinet, and shut the drawer. He walked out of the office and pulled the door closed behind him, making no effort whatsoever to hide the broken glass.

He'd have to run away, that's all there was to it. He could take the other four with him. They'd just have to take their chances. They could head to the city.

Luke had lost all track of time, now. Before he woke the others and terrified them out of their wits, he decided, he'd peek outside and see how much time they had left before daylight.

He went to the door they always used, the one that led to the woods and had once led to his garden. He tried to turn the knob, but his hand must have been weak with exhaustion. His fingers slipped right off. He gripped the knob again, and tried harder.

The door was locked. Locked from the outside.

Panicked, Luke ran to the front door, the one he'd come through with Mr. Talbot that first day.

It was locked, too.

What kind of a school kept its students locked in, at night?

No school. Just prisons.

Luke rushed around trying every door he could find, but it was hopeless. They were all locked. And none of them had glass panels for him to break.

Finally he sank to the floor outside his history classroom.

We're trapped, he thought. *Trapped like rats in a hole.*

Luke was not the least bit surprised when he heard footsteps coming down the hall. He hardly dared look up. But it wasn't Jason or someone from the Population Police standing over him. It was his history teacher, Mr. Dirk.

"Back to bed, young man," Mr. Dirk said. "I appreciate your dedication to history, but studying through the night is strictly prohibited. I'm afraid I'll have to give you—"

"I know, I know," Luke said. "Two demerits."

Under Mr. Dirk's stern gaze, Luke resignedly trudged back upstairs.

CHAPTER THIRTY-FOUR

L uke was overcome by guilt when he woke up the next morning. How could he have slept away so many hours? He'd had to come back to his room because Mr. Dirk was watching. But he could have sneaked out later. Why hadn't he at least warned the others?

Some rational side of his mind argued: What good would a warning do when they couldn't escape?

Around him, his other roommates were complaining about the exams they faced that day. One or two of them had books open on their beds and were studying as they got dressed. It seemed unreal that anyone could care about exams at a time like this.

Fearfully, Luke looked over at Jason's bed. It was empty. The sheets were rumpled the same way they'd been last night. The pillow still held an indentation. But Jason was nowhere in sight.

"Where's Scott?" Luke asked. His voice trembled despite his best efforts to sound casual.

His question was met with blank stares.

"Don't know," one boy finally mumbled, and went back to studying.

At breakfast, Luke sat with Jason's gang, but Jason was still missing. Luke peered around the table at the four boys Jason had betrayed: Antonio/Samuel, who had flashing dark eyes and a quick laugh; Denton/Travis, who knew hundreds of riddles; Sherman/Ryan, who talked with an accent Luke had never heard before; and Patrick/Tyrone, who had once claimed he got his fake I.D. by "the luck of the Irish." Luke couldn't have said he really knew any of them well. But it was agony to sit there watching them eat their Cream of Wheat, making jokes, totally unaware that they were doomed. Luke tried to lean over and whisper in Patrick's ear, "You're in danger—I need to tell you—" But Patrick only brushed him away with the words, "Quit it, lecker. You're bugging me." And then all the others stared at Luke. How many of them were on Jason's side, working for the Population Police?

Luke didn't dare give his warning out loud.

Breakfast time slipped away, with Luke's panic only growing. His thoughts ran in circles. He should go hide, by himself, if he couldn't save the others. But he couldn't just abandon the others. He had to save them. But how?

"If you're not going to eat your breakfast, I will," Patrick said when Luke's was the only bowl that wasn't empty.

Silently, Luke passed over his food.

"Hey, thanks," Patrick said, with a huge grin. "You're the greatest."

If only you knew . . . , Luke thought miserably.

Just then, the dining hall door banged open.

"Population Police!" a booming voice called out.

Luke froze. He'd known this was coming, but it still didn't seem possible. He tried to yell, "Run!" to Patrick and the others, but he opened his mouth and nothing came out. His legs were frozen, too. He could only sit and watch and listen in horror.

A huge man stepped into the room. Medals covered his olive green uniform. He clutched a sheaf of papers in his fist.

"I have a warrant here for the arrest of illegals who have compounded their crime by the use of falsified documents," he announced.

Luke closed his eyes, in agony. It was all over. He'd failed at everything. He hadn't saved the others, and he hadn't saved himself. He'd never done anything for the cause. He was going to die before he'd had a chance to accomplish a single thing.

The police officer peered at the papers in his hand. He cleared his throat.

"The sentence for those in violation of Population Law 3903 is death. The sentence for falsification of documents by an illegal citizen is death by torture, Government's choice."

One of the autistic boys was crying. Luke could hear him across the room. Everyone else sat in deathly silence. Luke hoped that he'd at least have the chance to apologize to the other four. The police officer continued.

"The first illegal I have come to arrest goes by the name of—"

"Relax, Stan. I found him," someone interrupted from behind.

Luke recognized the voice. A second later, Mr. Talbot came into the room.

And behind him, with his wrists in handcuffs and his ankles in leg-irons, was Jason.

CHAPTER *THIRTY-FIVE*

T he entire dining hall full of boys gasped.

"He was hiding in the nurse's office," Mr. Talbot was saying. "And the other one's over at the girls' school. Come on. I don't want to miss my golf game this afternoon."

"No!" Jason roared. Even in chains, he had a commanding presence. The police officer with the chestful of medals turned to look at him with something like respect. "I told you! I'm not an exnay. I can show you the exnays!"

Jason stepped forward, chains rattling. Mr. Talbot reached out to grab his arm, but the officer stopped him.

"Maybe he's right," the officer said. "I always love it when they betray each other. And I wouldn't mind getting a bonus for exceeding my quota this month."

Mr. Talbot shrugged and looked at his watch, as if all that worried him was showing up late for his tee time.

Jason hobbled slowly across the room, until he reached Luke's table. Luke felt faint. Everyone around him seemed to be holding his breath, too.

Jason pointed.

"Him. Antonio Blanco is his real name, but he goes by Samuel Irving. Him. Denton Weathers, alias Travis Spencer. Him. Sherman Kymanski, alias Ryan Mann. Him. Patrick Kerrigan, alias Tyrone Janson." Now Jason pointed to Luke. "And him. I don't know his real name, but he's pretending to be Lee Grant." He turned back to the Population Police officer, beseechingly. "And I know there are more. Just give me some time—"

Mr. Talbot started laughing. His guffaws rang out in the silent dining hall like bells after a funeral.

"Lee Grant an imposter? Now, that's a good one. I've known Lee since he was a baby. His whole family used to celebrate Christmas with mine, back when we lived in the city. Come to think of it, I've got one or two of those Christmas pictures in my wallet right now. Want to see them?" Mr. Talbot asked the police officer. He was already pulling the wallet out of his back pocket. "Hey, Lee, good to see you. Come look. Remember the year your parents made you wear the Santa Claus hat?"

Somehow Luke managed to make his legs carry him over to Mr. Talbot. Once before, Mr. Talbot had lied and said that he was a close personal friend of Luke's father's cousin. That was dangerous enough. Mr. Talbot could never back up this lie.

But the picture Mr. Talbot thrust at him was crystal clear. There was Mr. Talbot and three other adults, standing by a fireplace. Two boys that Luke recognized as Jen's brothers—Mr. Talbot's stepsons—sat on the hearth. And there, right between them, was Luke, in a flannel shirt and a Santa hat.

Mr. Talbot even flashed the photo in front of Jason's face.

"But I know—" Jason fumed. "He—I mean, I'm sure of the others. I'm positive!"

"Um-hmm," Mr. Talbot said. "I bet you just made up those names, trying to save your own skin."

Suddenly Patrick/Tyrone spoke up.

"He is, sir. My name is really Robert Jones."

"I'm Michael Rystert," Sherman/Ryan added.

The other two gave different names, too—Joel Westing and John Abbott. All four boys spoke in calm, even voices. Luke was stunned. What was going on? How could they possibly pull this off?

"They're lying! Look at their records!" Jason screamed.

"Good idea," Mr. Talbot said. "Is there a teacher or administrator who would be so kind—?"

At a far table, Luke's history teacher, Mr. Dirk, stood up.

"Just give me a minute," he said. Luke wondered how he could have ever found the man intimidating. He scurried out of the room like a mouse. In no time at all, he returned with four thick files. He handed them to the police officer. "Mind, please don't let any of the boys see. We like to keep their records private—"

But everyone was craning his neck, straining to see. Luke had the advantage because he was still standing next to Mr. Talbot. The police officer flipped quickly through the top file—Luke could see MICHAEL written again and again on each page. And in the next file, it was ROBERT, over and over and over.

"They're fake!" Jason howled.

"Aw, who could have faked these? In the two minutes we were standing here?" the police officer said in disgust. He threw the files down on the table and jerked on Jason's arm. "Come on. Out of here. Enough of your lies. We'd better go make that other pickup quick, or Mr. Talbot here will make me reimburse him for his lost greens time."

"But—but—" Jason sputtered, all the way out of the dining room.

And then he, and Mr. Talbot, and the Population Police officer were gone.

CHAPTER *THIRTY-SIX*

I t was strange, after everything that had happened, that the boys could shuffle off to their classes as usual. The hall monitors watched as usual. Once the bell rang, the teachers cleared their throats as dryly as ever and began lecturing about integral numbers or laws of thermodynamics or long-dead poets.

Luke took his history exam that afternoon, as scheduled. He was surprised that he could pencil in responses about Hercules and Achilles, Hannibal and Arthur, heroes of the distant past, even as his mind raced with questions about the present. He longed to ask Patrick/Tyrone—no, make that Robert now—for an explanation. Or any of the others. How had they known the right names to say? How had their records been changed? How was it that nobody in the entire dining room had stood up to challenge their stories? And—who had betrayed Jason?

But each time he saw the other boys, they only groaned about their exams, complained about the school food, told stupid jokes. They acted like their names had always been Michael, Robert, Joel, and John.

Nobody mentioned Jason.

"Are we going to the woods tonight?" Luke whispered to Trey as they were leaving dinner. "To talk about—you know."

Trey looked at him as though Luke was speaking a foreign language.

"Guess not, huh?" Luke said, unable to just let it go.

Luke felt an arm on his shoulder just then.

"I'd like a word with you, young man," a voice said.

With all his fears from breakfast-time rushing back, Luke had to force himself to turn around.

Mr. Dirk, his history teacher, stood there, looking stern.

"You are Lee Grant, are you not?" Mr. Dirk asked.

The other boys stepped past him. Luke watched the doors of the lecture hall close before he could bring himself to nod.

"Then come with me," Mr. Dirk said, and turned on his heel.

Luke followed a few paces behind. So Mr. Dirk was going to tell him how badly he'd failed the history exam. So what? Luke remembered that, with Jason gone, there was no one to doctor his grades. But Luke had never cared about the grades.

"I'll work harder next term," Luke started to say. "I didn't even start going to your class until last week—"

"Hush," Mr. Dirk said.

Luke fought the urge to giggle. It was so ridiculous that, after surviving the Population Police raid, he was getting in trouble because he had forgotten the names of a few dead guys most people had never heard of.

Mr. Dirk walked past his classroom. Luke started to protest, but Mr. Dirk was walking briskly now. Luke had to hurry to keep up. Mr. Dirk walked right up to the front door and turned the knob.

"Isn't it locked tonight?" Luke wanted to ask. But he was beginning to understand that Mr. Dirk wasn't going to scold him about ancient history. He kept his mouth shut.

The door opened easily. Luke and Mr. Dirk stepped outside together.

Tiers of steps lay before them in the twilight. Luke remembered his trepidation climbing these very stairs, his first day at Hendricks. They didn't seem quite so imposing now, probably because he was at the top looking down, instead of the bottom looking up.

"Where are we going?" Luke couldn't resist asking.

For an answer, Mr. Dirk put a finger to his lips.

They climbed down the steps and walked along the expansive driveway. June bugs sang, far off in the distance. They made Luke homesick. Back on the farm, his dad and brothers were probably just coming in for supper after a hard day of baling. Mother would just be getting home from the factory.

It didn't seem right that Luke had just had one of the most terrifying days of his life, and his own family would never know.

"Watch your step," Mr. Dirk said.

Luke had been so lost in thought, he hadn't even noticed that they had turned, and were now standing in front of a small cottage. No—not a cottage—the small scale had fooled him. This building had turrets and arches like a castle, but was nestled so neatly behind lilac bushes and rhododendron and forsythia that Luke could have walked right past without seeing it at all.

"Ring the bell," Mr. Dirk instructed. He turned to go.

Luke was swept with panic.

"Wait!" he cried. Mr. Dirk was hardly a comforting figure, but at least he was familiar. Luke didn't like being abandoned in a strange place, without explanation.

"I trust you can find your way back on your own, when you are finished," Mr. Dirk said, and disappeared into the shadows.

There was nothing for Luke to do but press the doorbell.

"Come in," a deep voice called from inside.

Luke gave the door a little push. It was made of the same kind of heavy wood as all the doors at Hendricks. It barely moved. Timidly, Luke edged it open and stepped inside.

A dim room lay before him. Prisms hung from old-fashioned lamps. Wood-framed couches curved between oddly shaped tables cluttered with dozens of framed pictures. Luke didn't even notice the man in the wheelchair until he cleared his throat.

"Welcome, young man," the man said. He was older than either Luke's parents or Mr. Talbot. He had thick white hair that swelled above his forehead like a snowbank. He wore crisp khaki pants and a pale blue shirt—the same kind of Baron clothes Luke had almost become accustomed to wearing himself. "Would you care for a drink? Bottled water, perhaps?"

Luke shook his head, baffled. Questions swarmed in his mind.

"George," the man called.

Mr. Talbot stepped into the room from the back part of the house.

Luke's knees went weak with relief. Finally! Someone who could explain.

"Mr.—" Luke began.

But Mr. Talbot shook his head warningly. He waved a long bar in front of Luke's chest and his legs, then behind his back. Finally he leaned back and announced, "He's clean. No bugs."

"I hate all this technology, don't you?" the man in the wheelchair said, leaning back as though Mr. Talbot's announcement had freed him to relax. He stirred a cup he held in his hand. Luke thought he caught a whiff of something like the chicory coffee his parents had sometimes drunk as a special treat. "But now I can introduce myself. I'm Josiah Hendricks. You know my friend here, I presume."

Luke could only nod.

"Sit down, sit down," Mr. Hendricks said. "No need to stand on ceremony."

Luke noticed that Mr. Talbot, always so much in charge every other time Luke had seen him, obeyed instantly. Luke quickly sank into an armchair as well.

Mr. Hendricks sipped his drink.

"You are an inquisitive young man," he said to Luke. "You wish some explanations. No?"

"Yes," Luke said eagerly. He looked over at Mr. Talbot, expectantly. But Mr. Talbot was staring pointedly at Mr. Hendricks.

"Once I was a very rich man," Mr. Hendricks said. "I spent my money foolishly—who doesn't when they have more money than they know what to do with? There is a long and not particularly attractive story about how I spent my younger days. But suffice it to say that I was given reason to develop compassion by the time of the Great Famines." He looked down quickly. Luke saw for the first time that both of his pants legs hung empty below the knee. "I am not disguising anything for you tonight," Mr. Hendricks said softly.

Luke shifted uncomfortably in his chair. What was he supposed to say? Evidently, nothing. Mr. Hendricks went on with his tale.

"You know the Government was considering letting the 'undesirables' starve, do you not?" Mr. Hendricks asked. "When there is not enough food, who deserves to eat? The blind girl? The deaf boy? The man missing his legs?"

The anger in his voice was unbearable. Luke stumbled over his own tongue, ready to say anything to move the story along.

"Jason—I mean, the one taken away this morning—he told me about that. At school."

"Indeed," Mr. Hendricks said. He seemed lost in thought, then roused himself to continue. "My family— and I—spent millions on bribes, to convince the Government to have a heart. They left the disabled alone. And passed the Population Law instead." He frowned, stir- ring his coffee. "And how compassionate had I been? I saved my own kind, knowing that others would likely be killed. So I set up the schools. As penance."

"Mr. Hendricks foresaw what others did not," Mr. Talbot said. "He understood that hundreds of illegal children would be born, and hidden. And he knew they'd need safe places to go if they were able to come out of hiding."

"But I thought your schools were for autistic kids, kids with phobias, the ones who—" Luke stopped. "Oh," he said.

Mr. Hendricks chuckled.

"So my charade fooled you?" he asked. "Who can tell if a child rocks because he has autism or because he is terrified out of his wits? Who can tell if agoraphobia is caused by oddities in the mind or lifelong warnings, 'Going outdoors is suicide'? In the beginning, yes, I accepted children whose problems stemmed from other causes. I nurtured a reputation as a schoolmaster who would take on any trou- bled child. And when the first illegal children began emerging, they came here, too."

Luke tried to grasp it all.

"So everyone's an exnay? And everyone knows?" he asked. "The teachers, Ms. Hawkins in the office, the nurse, all the other boys—"

"Oh, no." Mr. Hendricks shook his head emphatically. "My charade is complete. I don't even know for sure which boys are which. I don't want to know. There is the possibility of—"

"Torture," Mr. Talbot said grimly.

"Those I don't know, I can't betray," Mr. Hendricks said. "And I hire only employees who seem uniquely capable of ignorance. Teachers so enamored of their academic disciplines that they can't even recognize the students who sit before them for an entire year. Administrative staff whose incompetence is of such towering magnitude that they can't input records into computers, won't notice when files are faked or replaced. . . . There's a certain charm to my system, is there not?"

Luke remembered how Jason's portable phone had disappeared, how the doors had been locked, how the files under his four friends' new fake names had magically appeared.

"But *someone* knows," he insisted. "There has to be *someone* who oversees it all."

Mr. Hendricks shifted in his wheelchair.

"Oh, yes. I have my compatriots. Mr. Dirk, as you probably suspect, has been useful upon occasion, although his knowledge is limited. I will tell you no other names."

Luke should have felt relieved to finally get an explanation. For that matter, he should have been ecstatic to have an adult at Hendricks acknowledge his existence. But all he could think about, suddenly, was how lonely and isolated he'd felt his first few weeks at Hendricks, how invisible. How low he'd sunk, that he'd almost looked forward to Jason picking on him each evening. He felt a surge of anger.

"You think you're so great," he said before he could stop himself. "Don't you know how it feels to be an exnay? And then you just abandon us, among people who don't care. Or can't care. It's a wonder we don't all run back into hiding."

"Oh, no," Mr. Hendricks said, seeming totally unruffled by Luke's outburst. "You were never abandoned. I can assume you have never been deep-sea diving, correct?"

Luke shook his head, and resisted the urge to roll his eyes as well.

"But you understand the concept?" Mr. Hendricks didn't wait for a reply. "When a diver resurfaces, he has to go gradually, so his body can get accustomed to the change in pressure. Children coming out of hiding need that, too. They need places to adjust to the outside world. Somewhere that their extreme fear of the outdoors does not seem out of place. Somewhere that they can act antisocial and not stand out. Somewhere—well, like Hendricks. And then when they're ready, they move on."

"You mean—leave?" Luke asked, his voice squeaking in spite of himself.

"Yes," Mr. Talbot said. "And Mr. Hendricks and I agree: The events of the past twenty-four hours prove that your time has come. You're ready to go."

CHAPTER THIRTY-SEVEN

"**H**uh?" Luke said. He had not anticipated that turn in the conversation at all.

Mr. Hendricks leaned forward.

"My schools had never been infiltrated before," he said, with a sharp glance at Mr. Talbot.

Mr. Talbot frowned apologetically.

"The Population Police have always pretended that it's impossible for an illegal child to get a fake I.D.," Mr. Talbot added. "But after the rally—" His eyes clouded. Luke could see the effort he was making to continue without emotion. "After the rally, all the rules changed."

"So you see, we never expected betrayal," Mr. Hendricks said. "In the beginning, yes, we tiptoed and looked over our shoulders. And, fortunately, we kept habits of . . . strong security. But we were not prepared for the Population Police to plant impostors in our midst, to gather names, to encourage indiscretion."

Luke frowned.

"But Jason—he said there'd been raids before. He said—"

Mr. Talbot had a sarcastic smile on his face. Mr. Hendricks raised one eyebrow.

"My dear boy," Mr. Hendricks said. "He lied."

Luke grimaced. He didn't like them acting like he couldn't figure that out on his own. But he'd learned a lot from Jason. What was true and what was false? He remembered one of Jason's other explanations: *You can't be too nice to an exnay . . . exnays need the kind of friend who can toughen them up. Like I did for you.* Luke remembered how many times Jason had made him claim to be an idiot, do push-ups until his arms collapsed, make a total fool of himself. Jason hadn't been trying to toughen Luke up. He'd been trying to break him down.

But it hadn't worked.

Luke didn't know why. He felt breathless, thinking about what could have happened. Suddenly he was mad at Mr. Hendricks and Mr. Talbot, sitting there looking so condescending.

"Why didn't you know Jason was an impostor?" Luke said. "You should have. He acted so different from everyone else."

"Yes, and so did you," Mr. Hendricks replied quickly. "Should we have suspected you of working for the Population Police, just because you liked going outside?"

Luke blinked.

"Yes, we knew," Mr. Hendricks said. "Just as we knew Jason, as you call him, was forming a club of former hidden children. We'd never seen that happen before, and frankly, we viewed it as a positive development. Until you showed us the truth."

Luke remembered how frustrated and frightened and alone he'd felt, only the night before.

"I didn't do anything," he said. "I tried, but nothing worked. Mr. Talbot deserves all the credit."

"You stopped the infiltrator and knocked him out. Then you took him to the nurse who, under the school's protocol, had to alert me," Mr. Hendricks said. "She thought he was just another former hidden child, going through some very unusual trauma. But when he muttered, "my phone, my phone"—she got suspicious. We locked all the doors and made a search of the entire school building."

So that's what Jason had muttered to the nurse, Luke thought. He was kind of glad now that he hadn't heard. He had felt panicked enough, as it was.

"Once we confiscated his phone," Mr. Hendricks continued, "we found out that the last number he called was the Population Police. Meanwhile, your call made George here suspicious—"

"Without spilling everything for the bugs on my phone, thank you very much," Mr. Talbot said. "Because of your warning, I had time to double-cross the Population Police's efforts. So we arrested two traitors, instead of six former hidden children. A good trade, in my mind."

Luke felt dizzy. No matter how many explanations Mr. Talbot and Mr. Hendricks gave him, other questions sprang up in his mind like so many weeds. Both men were watching him.

"Nina," Luke said finally. "Nina was the other traitor."

"Yes," Mr. Talbot said.

Luke thought about how, just for a second, he'd mistaken Nina for Jen that first night out in the woods. He'd wanted to like Nina so badly. He'd liked the way she'd laughed. But she'd been a traitor, too.

"What will happen to them?" Luke asked. "Jason and Nina, I mean."

Mr. Talbot looked away.

"Sometimes it's better not to know," he murmured.

That meant they were going to be killed, Luke thought. Killed or tortured to death, which was even worse. He shivered. Was it his fault? Was there some way he could have saved the other exnays without destroying Jason and Nina? No—they were the ones who had chosen betrayal.

"This is a cruel business," Mr. Talbot said. "Don't dwell on it."

In a corner of the room, an old-fashioned clock ticked quietly. Luke gathered his thoughts for his next question.

"But why did the Population Police believe you instead of Jason? If he'd wanted to, that officer could have arrested us all," Luke said. He remembered how careful Mr. Talbot had had to be, ever since the rally, for fear that someone might connect him with Jen. "I thought you were out of favor at Population Police headquarters right now. No offense, of course," he added quickly.

Mr. Talbot shrugged, as though being out of favor was as insignificant as a mosquito bite.

"I had the evidence on my side," he said. "They like

evidence. And I have to say, it was a stroke of brilliance to computer-enhance that Christmas picture, to substitute your face over Jen's." He kept his voice even, saying Jen's name, but Luke noticed that Mr. Hendricks bowed his head, reverently, as though giving in to a moment of silent mourning. Had Mr. Hendricks ever even met Jen? Luke didn't know, but he found himself lowering his head as well.

"Jen would have liked that," Luke said. "Using her picture to fool the Population Police." He swallowed what might have been a giggle. Jen would have been very amused.

"And what better way to remember those we love than by doing what they like?" Mr. Hendricks asked.

Mr. Talbot nodded, silently. Mr. Hendricks took over the explanation.

"And, young man, you do not realize the power of the name you have been given. Lee Grant. Your father—the father listed on your school records—is a very important man in our society," he said.

"But he's not my father," Luke said, more forcefully than he intended. "I've never even met the man. And I'm not Lee Grant."

Mr. Hendricks and Mr. Talbot exchanged glances. Luke wondered if they were deciding he wasn't so ready, after all.

"But you know how to pretend to be Lee Grant," Mr. Hendricks said. "That is what matters."

Luke shook his head impatiently. He'd suddenly had it

with all this double-talk. None of this was real, not the way planting potatoes was, or growing beans. It was easier to be a farmer, to know by looking whether your crops were good or not. Still, another question teased at the back of his mind.

"Why did they do it?" he asked. "Jason and Nina—why did they betray their friends? Their fellow exnays?"

"They were never your friends," Mr. Hendricks said harshly. "They came to Hendricks and Harlow schools with one purpose, and one purpose only: to seek out and betray all the former hidden children they could. They preyed upon all the exnays' secret desire to speak their real name, because the Population Police needed the real names to complete the betrayal. Jason and Nina had never been hidden children. They were just plants. Impostors."

"But the Population Policeman said they were illegals with false documents—" Luke said.

"The Population Police can lie, too," Mr. Hendricks said grimly. "It suits the Government's purposes to say they are arresting third children rather than traitors."

Luke tried to absorb this. Nina, who spoke so passionately about the third children's cause; Jason, who talked about protecting exnays at Hendricks—they had never been in hiding themselves? They only wanted to harm the ones who trusted them most?

This was a level of evil Luke never could have imagined before, back on the farm.

And now Mr. Hendricks and Mr. Talbot wanted him to

go to another new place, someplace even more challenging than Hendricks?

"With all due respect to my friend here," Mr. Talbot nodded toward Mr. Hendricks, "we don't really know how Jason and Nina came to work for the Population Police, or why they came to these schools. We're mostly guessing. They're just kids, after all."

"'Just kids?'" Mr. Hendricks protested. "You think only adults are capable of such villainy? Naturally, adults must have put them up to it, but—"

"I'll be interrogating both of them tomorrow," Mr. Talbot interrupted quietly. "Let's just say I intend to discover facts that my Population Police colleagues probably don't want me to know. It's likely that those two kids were offered substantial bribes for their work. Or"—he laughed bitterly—"maybe they were true believers devoted to their cause. Who knows?"

Luke wondered about that. Long ago, when he'd first met Jen, he'd wondered if the Population Law *was* correct, if maybe he really didn't have any right to exist, to eat food that might go to others. But Jen had convinced him that wasn't so, that everyone had a right to live. No matter what. But what if Jason and Nina had truly believed in what they were doing, even among their enemies—just as Mr. Talbot believed in what he was doing, double-crossing the Population Police, even as he worked in their head-quarters every day?

Luke rubbed his temples. This wore his brain out even

more than the history test had. He wished everyone could just be what they were, and not have to pretend.

The clock in the corner began donging, giving off dis-tinguished, silvery peals. Luke read the time effortlessly, without having to count dongs: eight o'clock.

"Well," Mr. Talbot said, rising, "you'll need to get your things out of your room before the other boys come out of—what do you call it? Indoctrination? And then I can drive you to your next school tonight. I'll tell you about it on the way."

"No," Luke said.

Mr. Talbot and Mr. Hendricks looked at him in baffle-ment. Then Mr. Hendricks chuckled.

"Oh, so you boys have come up with another name for it besides Indoctrination?"

Luke understood the old man's confusion. He could go with that, make up some silly name for Indoctrination, pre-tend that that was all he'd been objecting to. But it wasn't.

"No," Luke said firmly. "I mean, I don't want to leave Hendricks."

Now Mr. Talbot and Mr. Hendricks absolutely gaped at him, thoroughly aghast. Luke could tell what they were thinking: *We gave him a new identity. We gave him a place to hide. We saved his skin today. And now he tells us "no"? How dare he?*

Luke gulped. He wasn't so sure how he dared, either. Only two months earlier, when he'd left home, he'd been a scared little kid afraid even to speak. He'd had a borrowed name and borrowed clothes—nothing but memories to call his own. But those memories were worth something, and so was he. He wasn't some pawn to be moved across a chessboard, according to other people's plans.

Luke thought about what he'd accomplished at Hendricks—not just what he'd done to help outsmart Jason, but what he'd done making his garden, trying to make friends, studying for his tests. *Jen, you'd be proud,* he thought. He tried to figure out how to explain to Mr. Hendricks and Mr. Talbot.

"I'm glad you want to help me," Luke started softly. "And I'm, um, honored that you think I'm ready to leave. But I don't think I'm done here. When I came out of hiding I told my parents that I wanted to help other third children. Only, I didn't know how. But now I do. I want to help them *here.*"

Mr. Talbot and Mr. Hendricks exchanged glances. Then Mr. Talbot sat down.

"Tell us more," he said.

CHAPTER *THIRTY-EIGHT*

T he sun was barely over the horizon, but it was already
a steamy day. Luke brushed sweat out of his eyes and
pushed another seed into the ground. It was late in the sea-
son to plant a garden, but they'd had to wait until after
exams. Luke could only hope for a late frost in the fall.

Behind Luke, four other boys clutched a sturdy rope
stretched across the garden rows. One boy dipped quickly
toward the ground, dropping a seed before he straightened up.

"Good, Trey," Luke said, laughing. "But it's easier if you
open your eyes."

"I might see something that way," Trey grumbled.
"Everything's so bright out here."

"Just smell, then," Luke suggested.

Trey breathed deeply.

"It's so fresh," he said in a marveling voice.

"Wait until you taste the peas you're planting," Luke said.

Luke was still surprised that Mr. Hendricks and Mr.
Talbot had agreed to his plan.

"I never intended to run an *agricultural* school," Mr. Hendricks had grumbled. "Some of these boys are from the

richest families—or supposedly from the richest families—"

"Then they need to know how food grows, as much as any-one," Luke answered, surprised at his own tone of authority.

Sometimes Luke wondered if he was just taking the easy way out—staying at Hendricks because it was familiar, grow-ing a garden because that's what he liked. But the Population Law had started over food, so nobody could say that growing food wasn't important. Or maybe that was the problem—that people had started believing it wasn't important.

Luke watched Trey plant another seed, this time with his eyes open.

"This little thing is really going to grow?" Trey asked incredulously.

Luke nodded.

"It ought to," he said. "And it'll be yours."

He hadn't been able to tell Mr. Hendricks and Mr. Tal-bot how much longer he wanted to stay at Hendricks school. Last week's exams had pointed out plenty of holes in his education, and he knew now that he could learn here. And, no matter what, he knew it had to be good for the other boys to get outside.

"Are you some kind of a teacher?" one of the boys behind Trey asked Luke. He spoke hesitantly, like a little kid just learning how to talk. "What's your name?"

"Just call me 'L,'" Luke said, without thinking.

Now, where had that come from? It wasn't Luke, it wasn't Lee—it was, somehow, both identities at once.

Just like Luke himself.